A Love Worth Waiting For

Waiting For

A Nearlake Novel

LARA VAN HULZEN

Happy Reading,
Lara Van Hulzen

MOSAIC PRESS

MOSAIC
PRESS

A Love Worth Waiting For
First Edition
© 2024 Lara Van Hulzen, All rights reserved.

www.laramvanhulzen.com

This is a work of fiction. The characters and events portrayed in this book are fictitious and otherwise imaginary and are not intended to refer to specific places or living persons. Any similarity to real persons, living or dead, is coincidental and not intended by the author. The author has represented and warranted full ownership and/or legal right to publish all the materials contained in this book.

ISBN 979-8-9914296-0-3 (paperback)
ISBN 979-8-9914296-1-0 (eBook)

Library of Congress Control Number: 2024918376
Printed in the United States of America

FOR JERRI GREENMAN

Thank you for teaching me how to quilt. Thank you for teaching me that quilting is much more than sewing. It's a community. It's laughter. It's creating together. It is friendship in its finest form. I adore you.

DEAR READER,

For those who live in Idaho, it's easy to figure out that Nearlake is fictional. It's a setting I created based on a mix of cities I have visited in the state, a place made up of the many things I love about the beauty of this place and the kindness of its people. I'm grateful I get to call myself an Idahoan.

Happy reading,
Lara

1

SADIE WOODS UNLOCKED the front door of her family's antique store, Get and Gather, and stepped inside. The sound of the little bell attached to the top of the door rang through the quiet. The scent of oak, wood cleaner, and a hint of dust filled her nose. She took a deep breath in and smiled.

Her friends teased her that dust wasn't exactly a desired scent for most people, but it represented history and family to Sadie. Hers, as well as the stories each item in the shop had to tell. Oversized chairs that had sat in front of family room fireplaces with a grandparent reading to a grandchild. Or a dining table that held countless tales of meals shared— laughter and love sinking into the wood over time. The antique store had been in her family for years; her grandparents owned and ran it first, then her aunt, and now it was Sadie's turn to operate it.

She'd lived in Nearlake, Idaho, all her life, and the store was her second home. Small-town life suited her, as did being a part of the store. Not everyone felt that way, like her mother, who'd left when Sadie was young, but it didn't matter. What mattered was that her Aunt JoJo had taken her in, loved her, and raised her in the town they both called home.

She dropped her keys into the purse slung over her shoulder and ran a hand over the top of a dresser under the front window just inside the door. Made of mahogany, it was solid. Handmade. Dated back to the 1930s. In her opinion, the phrase "they just don't make them like they used to" was accurate.

Although some considered her job monotonous, it wasn't to Sadie.

Each item had a history but also a future. One of her favorite parts of working in the store was seeing a customer's eyes light up when they found what they were looking for, the smile on their face as they took a lamp, an old typewriter, or a picture frame home. It was as if Sadie was helping that item find its next place in history.

Fall décor graced the shop; pumpkins of all sizes were scattered around, along with corn stalks, scarecrows, and vases filled with fall foliage. Sadie had a smile on her face from October through January. How could she not? The red, orange, and yellow leaves on the trees, the air turning crisp and cool. Summer had its charms, but nothing could beat the fall. Contemplative by nature, Sadie also appreciated that it was a time of year to look back and see all the good that God had provided throughout the year.

She crossed her arms and leaned against the dresser, her smile fading. This year, it seemed much more challenging to find the good. And she had looked. Aunt JoJo's cancer had turned life upside down. Between running the store and caring for her aunt, Sadie was exhausted.

Her mind drifted to the letter inside her purse, and her heart sank. A few days ago, she'd received notice that the landlord was raising the rent. She was praying about all of it, but her hope was fading. She hadn't told Aunt JoJo anything. The last thing she needed right now was something that huge to worry about.

She moved away from the dresser and hitched her purse up higher on her shoulder. It wasn't time to wallow in worries. She had a shop to run. Lots to do. And she could do it. She *could*.

Making her way to the small office in the back, her spirits lifted. Yes. She could do this. She could nurse her aunt back to health, keep the store running, *and* find a way to pay all the bills—a piece of cake.

Her sneakers squeaked on the polished wood floor as she stopped short, her heart pounding. Standing a few feet from the shop's back door, she saw shards of glass on the ground.

Her eyes moved from the glass to the door. The top half of the door had once been a decorative piece of stained glass, but it looked as if someone had punched a hole dead center, the mosaic of colors now a mass of sharp and angry shards.

"What…?"

Fear, anger, and anxiety all rushed through her system as tears threatened to form in Sadie's eyes. She blinked them away.

Frozen where she stood, her mind raced. She looked around. There didn't seem to be any signs of disruption. The area near the back door was as clean as when she'd locked up and left last night.

Grabbing her phone from the back pocket of her jeans, she called the police. After one ring, a woman answered and said they'd send someone immediately. Sadie hung up and then took a few photos of the door, the floor, and the surrounding area on her phone. She still hadn't moved her feet. She'd read enough books and watched enough shows to know that touching anything or moving things was not a good idea.

It didn't take long before she heard a car pull up in front of the store. The bell dinged, and she turned to see the local Deputy Sheriff standing in the doorway.

Not just the Deputy Sheriff. James Larsen, to be exact. *The* James Larsen. The one she'd gone to high school with.

The one who was a football star, not just then, but through college and then the NFL. The guy she'd had a crush on all four years, but her being the shy, nose-in-a-book-wallflower-with-glasses-whose-name-he-didn't-know girl, they didn't exactly hang out.

"Sadie? Are you okay?"

Okay. Well, he knew her name now, apparently.

"I'm fine. But the back door is smashed, and I think someone broke in."

"Are you hurt?" He closed the door behind him and moved toward her.

"No. I'm fine."

"Good. You seem sort of...frozen in place, though. You sure you're okay?"

He stood beside her. His six-foot-four frame had taken up the doorway and now towered over her, his blue eyes searching hers for answers. She blinked, thrown off balance by his presence and cologne, which smelled like a mixture of pine and oak.

It didn't matter that it had been over twenty years since high school; any time she'd seen James around town, the shy girl she'd once been showed up. He still looked a lot like he had as a teenager, but now with a dusting of gray around his temples. His eyes didn't sparkle quite like they used to, dimmed by grief and bracketed by lines that said he carried pain. Sadie had heard about his wife's death but didn't know much.

"Sadie?"

Snap out of it, Woods.

She blinked. "Yes. Yes." She turned her attention to the back door and said, "I didn't want to touch anything or move anything in case I compromised an investigation."

When she turned back to him, holding up her phone to show him the photos she'd taken, she noticed his lips pressed together to suppress a smile, although one side of his mouth was lifted in what looked like a smirk.

She narrowed her eyes. "What?"

He shook his head. "Nothing. It's just the way you said, 'compromised an investigation.' Sounds like you know what you're talking about."

With one hand still holding her phone out, the other propped on her hip, she said, "You're making fun of me."

Now, he did smile. A full-on grin that did all kinds of crazy things to her insides. "No, ma'am. I'm guessing you read a lot of mysteries or enjoy cop shows."

"And what if I do?"

Not saying anything in return, he smiled down at her, his eyes twinkling in a way that gave her a glimpse of the boy she used to know, and it made her knees weak.

She shook her head. "I took photos in case they could be helpful."

"Thank you. That is helpful." He stepped past her toward the door. "Is it okay if I take a look around?"

"Of course."

He looked at her standing in the same spot as when he'd arrived. "You can move now, Sadie. You won't compromise anything."

That quirk of his mouth happened again, causing part of her to want to stand there longer out of spite, but she decided against it. The desire to look around won out.

As he crouched near the broken glass by the back door, Sadie set her purse down and moved around the store, taking more photos. She would go through them later to see if anything had been damaged or stolen. Her emotions were playing tilt-a-whirl with her mind at the moment, and James Larsen's proximity was not helping.

Her anger rose with each click sound of the camera on her phone. Who would want to break into her shop? She couldn't think of anyone who would want to hurt her personally, and although Nearlake wasn't a tiny village, it was small enough for people to pay attention, with crime not being a particular problem.

James stood and walked through the shop, his eyes wandering over floors and surfaces. "Is the window the only thing broken? Are you aware of anything missing?"

He stopped and put his hands on his hips as he faced her. By the way his uniform stretched across his chest, it was clear he worked to maintain his football-player physique.

Sadie shook her head if only to get her thoughts straight. "No. Nothing looks out of place or gone."

James rubbed his chin with one hand and looked at the

back door. "It's odd that the window is broken, but the door is still locked. No sign of someone reaching in to open it."

Sadie frowned and walked to the back door. James joined her.

"I didn't notice that," she said as she looked closer at the knob. "I came in through the front, saw the broken glass, and called you…well, the police, right away."

"And then literally didn't move until I got here."

She looked at him. "You're teasing me again."

He shrugged and held up his thumb and forefinger with a small space between them. "Just a little bit."

She narrowed her eyes at him and placed her hands on her hips.

He held up both hands in a sign of surrender. "Okay. I'm sorry. No more teasing."

With a heavy sigh, she looked back at the broken window, her shoulders sagging as she dropped her hands to her sides. The cost of a new window was the last thing she needed right now. With medical bills stacking up and the rent letter in her purse that haunted her thoughts, the weight of it all pulled her down a bit more with each passing moment.

She prayed, trusted, and did all she could to stay positive, but more often than not, none of that felt like enough.

James put a hand on her shoulder. "Hey, I'm sorry. I didn't mean to tease so much. You were smart to call immediately and be careful not to touch or move anything."

"It's not that," Sadie said with a shake of her head.

He moved his hand away, the warmth of his comfort gone, leaving Sadie to feel again it was her against the world.

"What is it then?" His eyes searched her for answers, his attentiveness making her want to cry her eyes out while wrapped in his arms.

She blinked the image away and shifted her shoulders back, swallowing any emotions that might cause tears. Getting lost in the feelings of a high school crush was *not* what she needed right now. No, right now, she needed to take a deep breath, which she did, and focus on the shop, her aunt, and keeping her world in order.

"It's nothing. Well, it's this!" she said as she used both hands to gesture toward the back door. "It makes no sense, and now I have to get this window repaired. Gary gave it to my aunt as a gift, specifically for the shop."

"Gary Wall from the cabinet and glass shop?" James asked.

"Yes. He makes stained glass and… ugh." Sadie's shoulders dropped again. Gary was such a nice man. She hated having to tell him the beautiful window he'd made was destroyed. He'd also had a thing for her aunt for years, asking her out and never getting past a close friendship. When Sadie questioned JoJo about why she wouldn't date the guy, her aunt would simply say that he was nice but not her type. Since JoJo had never married, Sadie wasn't sure what kind of man her aunt's type was, but she had to respect Gary's persistence. And it must have been love because he never married, either, accepting friendship from JoJo as enough.

James put a hand on Sadie's arm. "Hey. It's all going to be okay. Let me talk to Gary. I can explain what happened, and he'll understand."

"You would do that?"

"Absolutely. You focus on getting this covered as soon as possible." He turned and looked around the shop. "If it's okay, I want to look around some more, but then I'll help you get cleaned up so you can open the shop for the day."

Sadie stared at him. "You don't need to do all that. I'm sure you have more important things to do."

He smiled at her. "Sadie, I want to help."

She nodded. "Okay. Thank you."

After grabbing her purse, she went into the office. She plopped down in her desk chair and blew out a breath as she tossed her phone down on the desktop. Fumbling through her bag, she found the letter from her landlord and shoved it into the top desk drawer. Her aunt didn't have the strength to come into the store anymore, so keeping it there meant a better chance of JoJo not finding it and, therefore, worrying about it.

She stowed her purse in the bottom desk drawer and leaned her elbows on the desk, her head in her hands, in a vain attempt to hold together the emotions and thoughts that now swirled through her mind. No stranger to life changing on a dime, Sadie had experience adjusting quickly, but the past year had so many twists and turns that she found herself praying she could park on the side of the road for a while.

"I just need to catch my breath, Lord," she whispered.

The sound of the bell above the front door drew her from her thoughts. Her friend and employee, Moira, had arrived, the murmur of her voice mixing with James as he explained what had happened.

Sadie came out of the office to join them, and Moira raced to her, pulling her into a hug. "Are you okay? This is so awful. And so scary."

"I'm fine, Moira. A little shaken, but I'm fine."

Moira pulled back from the embrace and looked at Sadie. A close friend to JoJo and about the same age, Moira had worked at Get and Gather for years. "I'm so glad. The Deputy Sheriff was just telling me what happened."

They turned to look at James, who stood near the back door, broken glass by his feet.

"I'll go get what we need to clean that up," Moira offered.

Before Sadie could protest, Moira whisked by her to the storage closet where they kept cleaning supplies.

Sadie faced James. "Thank you again."

"Of course." He nodded. "I think I found something that might explain what happened."

"You did?" Sadie stepped toward him as he opened his hand to reveal a baseball.

"My guess is that some kids were playing in the alley

and hit the ball through your window. That would explain why the door was still locked and nothing touched inside."

Sadie stared at the ball in his hand. Relief flowed through her system that it wasn't an attempted burglary, followed by irritation that the kids who had broken the window hadn't owned up to their actions.

He put the ball in his jacket pocket. "Although it still isn't fun to deal with the window, I think it's safe to say no one is after your store or any of its contents."

Sadie nodded in agreement. "I think you're right. And I'm glad you found the ball."

He looked at the ground covered in glass and then back to Sadie. "I really am happy to help clean up."

"No, no. Moira and I can handle it."

"Okay. I'll contact Gary about the window." He moved through the store to the front door, Sadie following to walk him out. He turned as he opened the door, pulling a card out of his pocket. "That's my cell number. You call me anytime if you need anything."

"Thank you," she managed as he walked out and went to his squad car.

"Looks like you have your own personal knight in shining armor."

Moira's voice behind Sadie made her jump.

"Moira!" She turned and shook her head. "I do not."

Moira and Sadie looked out the front window to where James waved a hand as he drove away.

"Whatever you say, Sadie girl, but by the gleam in that man's eye when he looks at you, I beg to differ."

Sadie chuckled and shook her head. She turned the Closed sign in the window to Open and went to help Moira finish cleaning.

Her to-do list was a mile long, and one thing that she absolutely could not fit in was the time to daydream about James Larsen. He was the local law enforcement officer who came to help her; that was all. There was nothing between her and James, and she had no reason to believe there ever could be.

2

JAMES MANEUVERED HIS squad car through Nearlake. Although the town sat next to one of the largest lakes in the state, the locals joked that the founding fathers hadn't been all that creative when naming the town.

James hadn't been born and raised in Nearlake like a lot of others. He and his parents and brother moved there the summer before James' freshman year of high school and his brother, Mark's, eighth-grade year. His dad was a carpenter, and his mother was a retired attorney. After years in California, they'd moved to Idaho, wanting a smaller community for James and Mark. He was sure the fact that his father liked to go fishing and hunting had been part of the discussion when his parents made the decision, but whatever the reason, they'd come to Nearlake and never looked back.

James had left town for college and his years in the NFL, but once his daughter, Maddie, was born, he'd found he wanted the same things for her his parents had wanted for him. Maddie had been born at the end of his career, so she wasn't too influenced by the whirlwind that is a professional sports environment, and although that world had fit his wife, Tiffany, like a glove, he had been more than ready to leave.

Tiffany. They'd been married for eighteen years. She'd been gone for five.

The thought of her death still caused a lump to form in his throat, but not for the reasons people imagined. A car accident had taken her from him and Maddie, but Tiffany had left him emotionally long before that.

He rubbed his chin with one hand, the other guiding the car through downtown. It had been one heck of a day, and it wasn't even 10 a.m. yet. When the dispatcher called in about the supposed break-in at Sadie's shop, he wasn't far away and said he'd take a look. Although he had to admit there was more behind his willingness to take the call. The depth of his desire to race to her aid and protect her rattled him. Not one to typically offer to stay and help clean up broken glass, one look at the emotions she struggled to hide, and he'd been ready to move a mountain if it made her feel better.

Sadie Woods.

It wasn't as if he and Sadie had moved in the same crowd when they were kids. He was an athlete and had always had others swarming around him and Tiffany on his arm. But James knew Sadie. How could he not? Whenever he'd seen her curled up in a chair in the library reading a book or laughing with a friend at a table in the cafeteria at lunch, he'd been intrigued. She was genuine amid a sea of insecure teenagers fighting for attention. And she hadn't changed. The simple goodness that radiated from her was palpable. Beloved by everyone who knew her, she was the warmth of sunshine on a cold day. Her big, brown eyes a place James could get lost in for days.

He shook his head. What was he doing? Mentally waxing poetic about Sadie Woods would only lead to trouble. He was doing his best to *raise* a woman and a teenage one at that, which was confusing enough. The mere idea of dating came close to terrifying him. As if on cue, Old Dominion sang on the radio about the only thing they know about girls is not knowing anything at all. Wasn't that the truth?

And yet, it wasn't hard for his mind to drift back to Sadie. When he'd first arrived at her store, not knowing what the threat might be, his heart had raced in his chest when he saw her frozen in place. When she'd said she hadn't wanted to compromise an investigation, it took every ounce of self-control for him not to burst out laughing. But it was clear how serious she was about it, and making fun of her was not a good idea. In any other case, it annoyed James when people had certain ideas on how he should do his job based on shows they watched or books they read. It was called the "CSI effect" around the police station. But with Sadie, he found it endearing, as if she'd somehow been dropped into a Nancy Drew novel and wanted nothing more than to solve the case.

And yes, he knew all about Nancy Drew books. James' mother had given Maddie one for Christmas a few years back, and while most kids her age were glued to their phones, she spent most of her time with her nose buried in a book. Not unlike Sadie when she was younger. He smiled at the thought of how much Maddie would like Sadie.

It wasn't as if Maddie wasn't ever without her phone; she just didn't seem to have her face plastered to the screen all day, a small miracle James thanked God for every day. His gut clenched a bit at the main reason Maddie was good about her phone – Tiffany had been texting when she ran her car off the road and hit a tree. Who she'd been texting was information James would take to his grave, never telling Maddie, but he'd been unable to protect her from knowing that had been the cause of her mom's car accident.

He guided his squad car into a spot outside the police station, put it in park, and turned off the car. His mind was dealing with more emotion-driven thoughts than he'd had enough coffee to handle. The text tone went off on his phone. He pulled it out of his pocket, his hopes high that it might be from a message from Sadie.

It was his brother asking if he was free to grab a coffee together.

He smiled at the thought of Mark all but reading his

mind at his need for more caffeine and texted back, "Yes."

The Daily Grind coffee shop was only a block away from the police station, a brilliant move on the owner's part, in James' opinion. He locked his squad car, quickly checked in at the station, and headed down the street.

Mark was already at a table outside, his face turned toward the sun with a hand cupped around a large iced coffee. He was leaning back in his chair, one ankle crossed over his knee.

"Soaking in the rays with your girly drink?" James teased as he sat down in the chair across from his brother.

"You know it. Vitamin D and caffeine keep the doctor away."

James laughed. "I fear we need a lot more than that at our age."

Mark looked at him. "Hey, now. You're 45, and I'm 44. Far from old."

James nodded. "That's true. Although most days it doesn't *feel* true."

"Yeah. Well, I'll give you that."

James looked around. Five tables lined the windows outside the coffee shop, and two more were occupied. Through the window, he could see people working on laptops. One table had a couple cuddled together, reading papers on the table, while another had two women chatting while enjoying pastries and huge iced coffees.

The door to the shop opened, and one of the young

servers came over to them. "Hey, Uncle James."

He stood and hugged his niece. "Good morning, Mary."

Mark and his wife, Amber, had two kids: Mary, who was nineteen, and John, who was seventeen. When Tiffany died, Mark and Amber had been James' rocks. Mary and John had also taken Maddie under their wing. Yet another reason James was glad to be in Nearlake. Not only was it nice to have his parents close, but having Mark and his family for support was vital.

Tiffany had never been close to her parents. After high school graduation, they'd moved to Florida. They visited once a year to see Maddie, but that was all. James couldn't blame them. It had to be hard to come to a place filled with memories of the daughter they'd lost.

"Can I get you your usual?" Mary asked as James sat down again.

"I would love that, thank you."

"One manly coffee coming up." With that, she turned and went back inside with a smile and a swing of her long, dark ponytail.

"Tease all you want that my iced coffee isn't manly and your black coffee is, but I stand by my choices," Mark said as he lifted his cup in a mock toast and took a sip from the straw.

James laughed. "As you should."

"So, how are things so far on this beautiful fall day?" Mark asked.

"I had one call out to a robbery."

Mark sat forward in his chair and put his elbows on the table. "A robbery? Seriously? That's close to unheard of here."

"Yeah. It wasn't, though." James pulled the baseball from his coat pocket and held it up for his brother to see. "Looks as if some kids busted a window and ran." He put the ball back in his pocket. "At first glance, though, it did look as if the antique shop had been broken into."

"The antique store?" Mark asked. "As in, Sadie Woods' store?"

James nodded.

Mary came back with James' coffee and set it down in front of him. "There you go. Let me know if you need anything else."

"Thank you, Mary," James said, then took a sip and felt the much-needed flow of caffeine through his system.

Mark waited for Mary to go back inside before he said, "You mean the Sadie Woods you have a crush on?"

James set his mug down and shook his head. "What are talking about? A crush? We aren't 13."

Mark laughed and leaned back. "You totally have a crush on her."

"Okay, now I *do* know that girly coffee is getting to you."

Mark tilted his head, a sincere smile on his face. "It's okay to want to move on, James."

James nodded. "I know."

"Do you?"

He took a deep breath and leaned against the back of his chair. The sun warmed his skin and he closed his eyes. Did he know? He'd met Tiffany in high school and although she wasn't his first girlfriend ever, she had been the woman in his life for so long, he wasn't sure how to be with anyone else.

"You want to know what I think?"

Mark's question pulled James from his thoughts. He opened his eyes and looked at his brother. "Not particularly."

"I think you were interested in Sadie back in high school; you just never said anything."

James mentally chewed on that statement for a moment. His brother wasn't wrong. He had found Sadie interesting back then. But had there been more? As in, would he have dated her had he been given the chance? Hindsight is 20/20. He might change now what he could have done back then, but what did it matter? He'd made his choices, and they couldn't be altered.

"Your silence is quite telling."

"My silence tells you nothing beyond me not responding to your opinion," James said, then took another sip of coffee.

"Look," Mark said as he leaned his elbows on the table again, his face closer to James'. "I know better than anyone all the garbage you've endured so far in your lifetime. I'm not trying to tease you or give you a hard time. You're my brother; I love you and want you to be happy."

James nodded with a smile. "I know. I do. I just…" He shook his head.

"I get it. Raising a teenager is no joke. You worry about Maddie, you worry about Mom and Dad. You worry about me, Amber, and our kids. You worry about the people of this town. You worry about everyone but yourself. And I'm just telling you it's okay to want something for you."

Was that true? Maybe so, but James merely felt he was trying to do what was best for the people he loved. He'd spent years choosing himself. He had his pick of colleges to go to; he chose a life in the NFL when it was offered to him. A life that had its advantages, of course, but was also tough on his marriage and his family at times. Weren't all those years filled with him focused mainly on himself?

He was sure it was part of why he'd chosen to be a police officer. He wanted the rest of his life to be about others. To give to a community he cared about. To give his daughter as stable of a life as possible.

"I know what is spinning in that brain of yours, and I promise you that as scary as dating or allowing another woman into your life would be, it could very well be something positive rather than something negative."

James nodded. "I know you have my best interest at heart, but you're right. Dating sounds terrifying."

Mark laughed. "I'm with you on that. Much like you and

Tiffany, Amber and I married young, and I wouldn't want to be with anyone but her."

James had felt the same way. Which was what made it that much more painful when he and Tiffany drifted apart, and then he'd heard she'd been having an affair. It gutted him. He never claimed to be the perfect husband, but he truly had never loved anyone but Tiffany. He couldn't fathom being with anyone but her, even on their worst days. However, time had given him the ability to think, probably too much, about whether or not he'd created an ideal of what he wanted out of life and marriage but didn't listen enough to what her ideal had been.

So many mistakes and no way to rectify them.

"Okay, so. I didn't ask you to grab coffee so I could sit here and watch you beat yourself up in your mind."

James smiled. "Sorry."

"Don't be sorry. You've been through a lot. And you're a great dad. And brother. And son. I just hope and pray that at some point, you'll let loose a bit and see that maybe, just maybe, asking Sadie out could be good. You might even have some fun." Mark winked at him.

"I have fun."

"Ha!! I'm not talking about game night at Mom and Dad's or doing an escape room with Maddie – as fun as those events can be. I'm talking about fun with someone of the opposite sex. A date. Flirting. Laughter. A nice dinner, maybe some candlelight."

"Well, when you put it that way…" James smiled.

Mark stood. "While you're thinking about what I said, I'm gonna go grab a pastry. You want one?"

"Yes, please."

As his brother got them more coffee, James turned his face to the warmth of the sun once more. Maybe Mark was right – not something he would admit often to his brother—but the kind of evening he described sounded appealing. And the kind of night he hadn't had in a really long time. Certainly, it was the kind of evening he hadn't had with Tiffany in a while before her death.

He shook his head. He prayed for the day that Tiffany's memory wouldn't haunt him. And possibly a time when the thought of asking Sadie out on a date occupied his thoughts over how he could find redemption from the mistakes of his past.

3

SADIE PULLED INTO Sadie pulled into the driveway of the home she shared with her aunt. A small farmhouse just outside of town, it was the perfect size for the two of them. Painted white with a deck that wrapped all the way around the house, beautiful wooden steps led to the front door with windows on either side framed in the same maple wood as the door. The sun was beginning to set, causing the lights in the house to glow through the front windows, a beacon calling her home.

She turned off the truck and sat for a moment, not quite ready to go inside. While the house was normally her respite from the world, a place of quiet with lots of books and all the tea she could drink, it was becoming a reminder of all that was wrong with the world. Illness and financial strain saturated her thoughts lately, and no matter where she went, she couldn't seem to escape them.

She rested her forehead on the steering wheel of her truck; an eight-year-old Toyota Tundra JoJo had purchased for them to share, it being the perfect vehicle to transfer the furniture to and from the store. Taking a deep breath in and letting it out, she prayed into the silence of the car. "Lord, give me...Strength? Wisdom? A nap? I don't even know how to pray anymore."

True to his word, James had contacted Gary, who was more than happy to replace the window free of charge. He said the first one was a gift, so a new one would be as well; God bless the man. By the time she and Moira locked up for the night, they had the window boarded up in a way that would hold until Gary could install a new one. Grateful to everyone who'd helped her, as well as how smooth the whole process had gone, she still couldn't shake the fatigue that weighed her down.

Something as small as kids accidentally hitting a baseball through her window should be something that rolled right off her shoulders. And yet, her shoulders were already so loaded down, she feared the addition of one more small stress and she would fold like a house of cards.

It wasn't as if she went through life intentionally, wanting to be alone or handle things on her own. Though independent by nature, she really was more of a product of the hand she'd been dealt. Her father had never been in the picture. Pregnant and alone as a young woman, her mother had moved in with Sadie's grandparents. They'd passed away when Sadie was nine, leaving the house and antique shop to JoJo. Angry and bitter about how life had turned out, Sadie's mother had left and never looked back.

She shook her head. Her poor aunt. At twenty-one years old, she'd lost her parents, her sister, and inherited the family's business as well as a scared, confused nine-year-old girl. Only twelve years older than Sadie, JoJo had become more of a friend than a parent, and Sadie would literally be lost without her.

Sadie looked at the house. The silhouette of her aunt moved in the light behind the shutters that were slanted open a bit. How could she sit here feeling sorry for herself? JoJo had been handed so much worse in life than Sadie. Yes, it was awful to watch JoJo be sick, but it was happening to JoJo and not her. The woman had carried the weight of the world on her shoulders for most of her life and did so with grace. Sadie wanted so much to be just like her.

She grabbed her purse from the passenger seat and got out of the truck. Making her way into the house, she dropped her keys on the front table and hung her purse and coat on hooks near the door.

"I'm home!" she called out, even though she knew JoJo had probably heard her pull up.

"In here, Loves," Jojo called back. She'd called Sadie "Loves" for as long as she could remember.

JoJo said the same thing each evening when Sadie got home as if she wouldn't find her aunt in the lounge chair in the living room – the one place she was most comfortable.

"I made some soup for dinner," Jojo said.

Sadie's shoulders sagged. On top of everything, and with limited energy, her aunt was cooking for her. She went into the living room and gave her aunt a kiss on the soft skin of her cheek. Sadie noticed her eyes were bright. That was a good sign JoJo had had a decent day. "You didn't have to do that, you know?"

The murmuring of her aunt's favorite program played in the background. A series that was set in the early 1900s in a small town and appealed to JoJo, and to Sadie. It was full of history and interesting characters, not unlike Nearlake.

Her aunt smiled up at her. "I know. But when I do get a spurt of energy, cooking is one of the things I enjoy."

That was true. JoJo was a great cook. And made the best cookies, too. Sadie just wished the guilt would fade over her aunt doing any of those things when she wasn't feeling well. In the kitchen, she took the top off a pot and closed her eyes as she breathed in the scent of homemade vegetable soup. The aroma of onion and spices filled her senses. While dust was the scent of her days, JoJo's cooking was the scent of home.

Sadie grabbed two bowls from the cupboard and scooped soup into each one. Preparing a tray for JoJo, complete with a spoon, napkin, and a glass of water, she brought it into the living room and set it on her aunt's lap.

"Thank you, Loves."

"You are most welcome." She went back to the kitchen and made a tray for herself then sat on the sofa that was beside her aunt's chair. After settling in, she lifted a spoonful of soup to her mouth, savoring the flavor and how the meal warmed her from the inside out. The muscles in her neck and shoulders relaxed for the first time all day.

"Mmm. I know I made this, but I have to say, it's really good," her aunt said with a chuckle.

"It is delicious, and you can absolutely say that whether you made it or not."

JoJo smiled at her and then spooned more into her mouth. Sadie smiled back, glad to see JoJo in such good spirits. No matter what was happening, her aunt was a glass-half-full kind of person. But with the breast cancer diagnosis that had knocked them both sideways, Sadie could see there were times when it wasn't quite as easy for JoJo to have as bright a vision of life.

The doctors said that with a lumpectomy and radiation, they were optimistic they could get it all, and yet the possibility the doctors were wrong hung over Sadie like a dark cloud. JoJo was almost through her radiation treatments, and with the fatigue and nausea and how she was feeling overall, it was tough to imagine her vibrant, outgoing, cheerful aunt would fully return.

At five feet, three inches tall, and one hundred pounds

soaking wet, JoJo was already tiny. Between the surgery and radiation, she'd lost some weight, and there were times Sadie feared a strong gust of wind might blow her away. The soup turned in her stomach, her appetite gone. The mere thought of JoJo not being in her life tossed her emotions around like a rag doll. JoJo was the one person in Sadie's life who had never left her. Sadie couldn't bear the thought of her ever being gone.

"What is it, Sadie?" JoJo's smile had faded, a look of concern on her face instead.

Ever since she was a little girl, it had been close to impossible for Sadie to hide her feelings from JoJo. That didn't keep her from trying, though. Especially now.

"Nothing," she shook her head.

JoJo placed her spoon down on her tray and placed her hands on the arms of her chair. "You've stopped eating, and your eyes are heavy. I know you better than that."

"I'm just tired." Sadie spooned more soup into her mouth and forced a smile.

JoJo narrowed her eyes at her in suspicion for a moment but then picked up her spoon again and continued eating.

Sadie turned her attention to the television. "I love this episode."

"Me, too," JoJo said with a smile. "I just love when the Mountie comes rushing in to save her, and yet she's already dealt with the bad guy herself."

"Ah yes, the mix of a chivalrous act and an independent woman."

They both laughed.

"It's good to keep men on their toes," JoJo said with a wink.

"Is that right?" Sadie teased.

JoJo shrugged as one side of her mouth tipped up in a tiny smirk.

"What? What is going on with you?"

JoJo laughed. "Just that you try to avoid telling me what's wrong, and yet, I know everything."

Although it felt good to see her aunt have the energy to tease her, Sadie swallowed hard. Had JoJo found out about the rent? "Oh, really. Everything, huh?"

JoJo took a sip of her water and then leaned back in her chair. "Well, I know enough."

"Enough?"

"I know that the back window to the shop was broken. I know that a handsome police officer showed up and threw you off your game." She stuck out a finger as she ticked off each comment. "And I know that you are trying to keep all of it from me, but you can't because, as I said, I. Know. Everything."

Sadie's heart rate calmed. JoJo only knew about the events of the day, not the financial stress.

"You honestly think that Gary Wall and I don't talk? Or, for crying out loud, that Moira didn't text me the minute

James Larsen left the shop?

Sadie pinched her lips together. Of course. Sure, Sadie could keep the raising of the rent and even most of the stress over the extent of the medical bills hidden because her aunt was too worn out to go through the mail these days, but avoid the town gossip text thread? That was a force of nature few in town had ever been able to avoid, including Sadie.

"How often do you talk to Gary Wall?" Sadie asked, hoping the question would steer her aunt away from conversing about the window.

"Gary and I are good friends, you know that. And with him having to replace the window, he called me to ask if I wanted a specific kind or if he could surprise me."

"Did he now?"

JoJo waved a hand at her. "Stop it. You've been giving me a hard time about that man for years."

"And for years, I have wondered why you keep friend-zoning the man."

JoJo tilted her head and smiled. "From what Moira says, James Larsen sounds interested in you, and you won't even friend-zone him."

Sadie narrowed her eyes at her aunt. "Don't use my words against me. And James Larsen feels nothing for me. He was helping a citizen of the town, that's all."

JoJo laughed. "Suit yourself. But I think that man has had a crush on you since high school."

"Okay. You have lost your mind. James Larsen hardly

knew who I was in high school and hardly knows who I am now. On the other hand, Gary has had a crush on you for centuries."

JoJo wadded up her napkin and threw it at Sadie, which then bounced off her cheek and onto the ground. As both women laughed, Sadie's heart warmed. It had been way too long since the two of them had had an evening filled with good-natured ribbing and laughter. Moments that Sadie would never again take for granted.

Her aunt sighed and looked down at her bowl of soup. "This has been fun, but I am quite tired now. I think I'll tuck in for the night."

Like a wisp on the wind, the moment was gone.

"Of course, yes." Sadie stood and placed her tray on the coffee table so she could take the one from JoJo's lap. She put it in the kitchen and then returned to hug her aunt goodnight.

"Thank you again for the soup."

"You are so welcome, Loves. Get a good night's sleep. And stop worrying so much. You'll get lines in your face that have no business being there."

With a chuckle and a small wave, JoJo headed down the hall to her room and shut the door. Thankfully, the primary room of the house was on the main floor, so JoJo didn't have to do stairs. The upstairs consisted of two bedrooms, one of which was Sadie's and another which she'd turned into a combination library and home office. It wasn't a large space, but enough to hold a few bookshelves and a small desk under a window overlooking the side yard.

Sadie waited until she heard the soft click of JoJo's door before returning to her own tray of food. Her appetite gone, she took it into the kitchen and did the dishes then prepped the coffee pot to turn on in the morning.

She turned the television off and folded her aunt's blanket. It was fortunate both Sadie and her aunt were the early-to-bed-early-to-rise type. But these days, JoJo tucked in for the night even earlier than normal, leaving Sadie to fill the evenings vegging out to a television show, reading a book, or finishing up any work she may not have gotten to in the store that day.

She locked the doors and turned off lights. As she made her way up the stairs, she tried to do so quietly, but her feet felt heavy, each step an effort to not disturb JoJo.

Inside the office, she turned on the desk lamp and sat down. A stack of mail sat before her, a few days' worth she'd tossed there to deal with later. Looking out the window, she watched as the neighbors placed pumpkins on their front porch, the light from their front sconces glowing in the night.

Jan and Evan were a couple in their sixties who'd moved to Nearlake in retirement. Jan checked in on JoJo during the day and had brought them meals many times. They were a true blessing to have next door. They laughed as Jan tried to carry a large pumpkin, only doing so was close to impossible since she could hardly see over it. After kissing her cheek, Evan took it from her, his tall, broad frame able to carry it easily.

What must love like that feel like? Sadie had dated in college and was even serious with one guy to the point of considering marriage, but it had faded as soon as she said she wanted to live in Nearlake for the rest of her life. That seemed to shut down relationships pretty fast. Although she meant it, was living in her hometown an easy excuse to get out of commitment?

JoJo had never committed to marriage. In the few times they'd discussed it, JoJo said she hadn't met the right person, but deep down, Sadie wondered if it was because of all the responsibilities JoJo had. Had JoJo chosen to raise Sadie and run the store over love? Sadie hated to think she was the reason her aunt would live life alone, but was she doing the same thing?

Rubbing her eyes, she took a deep breath and grabbed her letter opener from the top drawer of the desk. Even though she wasn't sure how to pay all the bills, going through them and getting organized might help inspire her to find a way.

Sadie considered herself a glass-half-full person as well. Unfortunately, these days it felt as if her glass held merely a few drops, and she was too exhausted to think of how to fill it up again.

4

SADIE OPENED THE door to Lily Pad Café and stepped inside. Seeing her friend, Charlie, already at their favorite table lifted her spirits. However, her spirits were already much better that morning after hearing the pastor at church preach on hope. Afraid she had way too little of that these days, it was a good reminder that God cared for her, and she could place her hope in Him.

Sunday brunch at Lily's was a tradition she and Charlie and Anne had started years ago. Best friends since high school, the three of them had stayed close, Sundays being a perfect way to get together. Get and Gather didn't open until noon, Sadie wanting all her employees to be able to attend church, yet still have the shop open for tourists in town for the weekend.

Sadie's heart sank a little at the thought that Anne had been absent from their lunches for so long; it really was more just a tradition now for her and Charlie. Anne married a wealthy man named Leo, whom she met about fifteen years ago through mutual friends. They traveled the world, and Anne did not return to Nearlake often. If ever, really. The friends kept in touch via text and phone calls, but it wasn't the same. They even tried to have Anne join them via video call, but that didn't last.

"Hey, you," Charlie said as she stood and hugged Sadie.

"Hey, yourself." Sadie took her coat off and placed it on the back of her chair before sitting across from her friend.

"I know we chat all week, but sometimes a week feels like a year," Charlie said.

"I agree. Sorry. I know lack of communication is my weakness."

Charlie shook her head. "There was zero shaming in that comment. Just trying to say I miss you and I am beyond ready to talk and eat for hours."

Sadie smiled, "Me too."

"How are my two favorite, extremely loyal customers today?" Lily said as she walked up to their table.

"Doing great, Lily. How about you?" Charlie asked.

As the two women talked, Sadie felt a tinge of envy toward her friend. Charlie had married her high school sweetheart, Davis, and they had two beautiful children. Gabby graduated recently from college and lived in Boise, and Eli was in his second year at Boise State. Charlie and Davis were married for almost twenty-five years and were the epitome of what a healthy relationship looked like. Over the years Sadie had wondered if she would ever find what her friend had. Anne, too. Sadie didn't know as much about Anne's husband, having only met him a couple of times, but based on photos and updates, Anne's married life was blissful as well.

For the most part, she didn't have time to think about men or relationships, her life busy with the shop and volunteering and giving back to the community she loved so well. But now and then she had a twinge of curiosity of what her life might have been like, or would be like, if she found the right guy.

The thought of James Larsen not only knowing her name but teasing her, as well as being so helpful, came to mind. Her cheeks flushed a bit, so she took a sip from the water glass that sat in front of her.

"You two relax while I get your standard orders placed for you," Lily said, then headed towards the back of the café.

"Okay, spill it," Charlie said. She leaned back in her seat, her legs crossed and her hands in her lap. Her long dark hair was twisted up perfectly and held with a long clip on the back of her head. The bright blue blouse she wore made her dark brown eyes stand out, and if Sadie wasn't mistaken, they were twinkling a bit.

"Spill what?" Sadie asked, guzzling more water.

Charlie laughed out loud. "You are horrible—and I mean horrible—at hiding your thoughts. Or feelings."

Sadie narrowed her eyes at her friend. "Ugh. Not you, too."

"If you mean I, too, know that our handsome Deputy Sheriff was at your shop yesterday helping you with a broken window—which I want details about later—then yes. Me, too."

Sadie shook her head. "I do so love this town, but…"

"But the rumor mill is tough. Agreed. I'll say that I only know about it because Davis talked to Gary Wall about some windows for a project; Gary told him what happened, so then Davis asked me if you were okay. When I told him I hadn't heard from you, I figured you were fine."

Sadie's shoulders slumped, her hands resting on the table. "I really am so sorry. I didn't have two seconds to spare yesterday, or I would have reached out to you."

Charlie leaned forward and put a hand on Sadie's. "Hey. We have known each other long enough for me to realize that was exactly what was happening. I knew you'd call if you needed me, and I knew we'd see each other today, and I would get all the details face to face."

"You're the best friend ever, you know that?"

"Yes. Yes, I do." Charlie patted Sadie's hand and leaned back in her chair again as Sadie laughed. "And because Davis is a local contractor and Gary does windows and glass and because I volunteer at the high school library and have chatted with James' daughter, Maddie, and we all went to high school together, and Moira practically has a town texting hotline, we are all intertwined in a crazy, beautiful, and sometimes annoying way."

"You make it sound like some lovely mosaic rather than the rumor mill that it is."

"You and I both know that people in this town care about each other, and that is why they're…"

"Nosy."

Both women laughed.

"Yes," Charlie said. "And to be fair, a broken window at a local business rattled other business owners, as well as residents."

Sadie nodded. "I was pretty thrown when I first saw the window. To know it was just kids hitting a wayward baseball brings peace of mind. Although I wish they would have just fessed up and told me."

Charlie shrugged. "It happened after you were closed. Maybe they still will."

Sadie nodded. That was possible. The last thing she wanted was for kids in town to be afraid of her. She'd be understanding about the whole thing. It would be nice for them or their parents to help pay for the window as well, but that could very well be a big part of the reason they didn't want to come to her.

"You said you chat with James' daughter Maddie at the library. What's she like?" Sadie asked.

"Hmm. I thought there might be a decent amount of curiosity about our fine friend, James," Charlie teased.

"You know our history better than anyone. If you can even call it that. He had no clue who I was in high school, and he barely knows my name now. I've just seen Maddie around town, and she seems like such a great kid. My heart goes out to her losing her mother so young."

Charlie's smile faded. "Yeah. I feel the same way. James is a good guy. He and Davis are still friends, and they sometimes grab a beer together. But to my knowledge, James doesn't say much about what happened with Tiffany, and as far as Maddie goes, just that she's doing well and is a great kid."

Sadie nodded, then took a sip of water.

"Maddie is a rabid reader. I'll say that," Charlie continued. "She gives me hope for future generations that not all of them have their heads stuck in phones and computers."

Sadie thought about how books had always helped her get through life. Reading was not only an escape. It was diving into worlds with characters that went through the same things you did. Worlds where a kid could feel understood, if even for just a short while. She herself had been drawn to characters like Ramona Quimby who was curious and sweet, yet always felt misunderstood or awkward. Or Nancy Drew who dove into mysteries and found what she was looking for.

"What does she like to read?" Sadie asked.

"I've seen her with mysteries as well as adventure stories. She seems to prefer those. I have to say, it sounds to me like James, as well as his daughter, have caught your eye."

Sadie shook her head. "Stop. I merely feel for the girl and wondered if there was a way to connect with her *if* I ever see her around town."

Charlie nodded. "Got it."

"Okay, enough about James Larsen. We have much more interesting things to talk about."

"Like?"

"Like, who will be at Homecoming."

Charlie rolled her eyes. "Everyone will be at Homecoming. Most of us who grew up and went to high school here never left. Or left and came back. So, it's really not so much of a Homecoming as it is a reunion every year."

Sadie chuckled. Charlie wasn't wrong. It still didn't keep her from hoping Anne would come back.

Reading Sadie's mind, Charlie said, "I haven't talked to her in weeks. Have you?"

Sadie shook her head. It wasn't uncommon to go for weeks without hearing from Anne with the travel schedule she and her husband kept. But it still left an ache in her chest to not hear from Anne as often as they used to.

"I saw her mom the other day. She hadn't heard from Anne in a while either. I just wish we could figure out what keeps her away so long," Charlie said.

Sadie agreed. Although the three women were thick as thieves as kids, Anne had drifted away in the years since leaving Nearlake. She made it sound as if her life was close to perfect but never shared many details with Sadie and Charlie. It hadn't been hard to see in their teen years that Anne's home life hadn't been pretty. Her dad was not a nice man, and Anne had made it clear that the second she could leave town, she would. And she had.

"Here you go, ladies," Lily said as she set their meals down in front of them. "Let me know if you need anything else."

Sadie leaned forward and took in the scent of cheese and onion. Lily made the best French Dip sandwich in the world, and it was Sadie's weekly treat. Her mouth watered at the mere thought of it. She dipped a corner in the au jus and took a bite.

"How are things at the shop?" Charlie asked, changing the subject. There wasn't much more to say when it came to Anne. That topic was all questions and no answers. "I mean, besides a broken window."

Although typically Sadie shared pretty much everything with Charlie, she hadn't indulged any information about her financial situation.

"They're fine," she answered once she was done chewing.

Charlie narrowed her eyes as if sensing Sadie was hiding something but didn't push. Instead, she took a bite of her salad and rolled her eyes before finishing said bite then saying, "I don't know how Lily can make something as simple as a salad taste so good, but this is amazing."

The two women ordered the same thing every single week, and every single week they had the same response to their meals. Sadie found the things she could count on, no matter how small, were anchors in the waves of her life.

"I mean, the broken window was upsetting. I showed up at the shop in the morning and found glass all over the place. But once James found the baseball, I was fine. Now, it's more of the inconvenience of having a broken window, having to get it replaced, and all that comes with that."

Charlie nodded. "How is JoJo?"

"She's fine."

"Lots of 'fine' going on in your life right now," Charlie said, her eyebrows raised.

Sadie laid down her fork and placed her hands on her lap. Charlie was a sister to her. Sadie trusted her with her life. What kept her from pouring out all her troubles, she had no clue. Burdening others with issues that were hers didn't feel right. She was a grown woman who could solve what needed solving.

Yes, talking things through with Charlie about other topics helped her process and even come up with ideas she wouldn't have thought of on her own. But this was different. Charlie couldn't help her find more money somewhere, take away medical bills, or keep her rent from going up.

Sadie had already begun a list of ways she could save money or handle the financial strain. Although it pained her to do so, selling the house was on the list. It broke Sadie's heart just to *think* about presenting the idea to JoJo. And that would, of course, mean Sadie would have to tell her aunt about the financial stress, which wasn't an option.

"It's all truly fine, Charlie. I have a lot on my plate, especially with JoJo being sick, but we will get through it."

Maybe if she said it enough, she would believe it herself.

"How are the kids?" she asked, then popped a French fry into her mouth.

As always, Charlie's eyes lit up at the mention of Gabby and Eli, and the change of subject was successful.

"They are great. Eli is doing well in school. He recently aced an economics test. Gabby is busy with work, and Tanner is getting his MBA.

Tanner was Gabby's boyfriend and, from what Charlie had told Sadie, a great guy and a good match for her daughter.

"I'm glad to hear things are going well for them. Will they be here for Homecoming?"

"I'm not sure. I think they want to be here for Christmas, so I will skip Homecoming and just come back in December."

As the two friends fell into a familiar rhythm of conversation, Sadie began to relax. This was what she needed. Not to talk about all that as wrong, but to spend time with Charlie focused on all that was right at the moment.

"Did Miss Agnes reach out to you yet?" Charlie asked.

"Not yet. What about?" Sadie took another bite of her sandwich and then leaned back in her chair.

"I think she's afraid to bother you, but she's curious…"

"About the Christmas quilts." Sadie snapped a finger as she remembered exactly why Miss Agnes would want to talk to her.

Agnes ran the quilting group at their church, a group JoJo had been a part of for years. One that made quilts for those in the community who had just had a baby or had lost a loved one. It was a way of wrapping love around those who needed extra care at certain times of life. JoJo had continued quilting as much as she could, but with her energy being low, she hadn't been up to helping get Christmas quilts done. Every year the group made them for people in the hospital. Sadie knew JoJo was working on one for a woman she met while doing radiation, someone with a much grimmer diagnosis than JoJo. But that one quilt was all her aunt could manage this year, so Sadie had offered to help do what she could in JoJo's place.

She was no whiz at quilting like her aunt or the other women in the group, but she was good enough to contribute in her aunt's absence.

"I keep telling her it's no bother," Sadie continued.

"She just knows you have a lot going on right now. She

appreciates you volunteering to help but doesn't want to overload you."

"I'll give her a call."

"I honestly don't know how you do it," Charlie said.

One of the waitresses came and refilled their drinks. After thanking her, Sadie said, "Do what?"

"Everything," Charlie waved a hand. "You run the shop, you take care of your aunt, you volunteer multiple places."

"I don't do any more than anyone else in town," Sadie said.

"That's not true, and you know it."

Sadie shrugged. "I spend time on what matters to me."

"And that is commendable. However, would it be so bad to maybe just toy with the idea of doing something for yourself now and then? Go on a date, maybe?" Charlie lifted an eyebrow, her mouth curved in a small grin.

"You just said it yourself. I don't have the time."

Charlie shook her head and laughed. "You're impossible sometimes."

"And you love me."

"And I love you."

Sadie took a sip of her drink, glad that Charlie let that subject drop. She had never been against having a man in her life, she just couldn't seem to find the right one for her. And whether James Larsen knew her name or not, or if there was any truth to him being interested in her, her life *was* full.

Dating and a relationship were the last things on her mind.

5

TWO DAYS LATER, Sadie stood behind the counter at Get and Gather. Two days later, Sadie stood behind the counter at Get and Gather. After her lunch with Charlie on Sunday, she'd spent the afternoon quilting with JoJo. The back of their farmhouse held a small space that was once a screened-in porch, but years ago, JoJo had closed it in and made it into a sewing room. JoJo was able to finish the quilt for her friend, and Sadie made a dent in the Christmas quilt she'd been working on. She was able to call and get caught up with Miss Agnes.

Some of Sadie's favorite memories growing up were of that room. Even the sounds reminded her of days she would be curled up reading in the living room, the whir of the sewing machine mixed with the hum of the small television

JoJo watched while she sewed, serving as Sadie's background noise. And then, on weekend afternoons, much like the one they'd just shared, where JoJo would teach Sadie how to follow a quilt pattern, the squares or rectangles or triangles always coming together to make a beautiful design.

Although she didn't get to quilt as often as she would like to, Sadie appreciated what it taught her. No quilt was perfect. Made by human hands, there were stitches here and there that weren't straight or sometimes a square got sewn in upside down. No matter what, each one became a thing of beauty—the end result exactly as it was meant to be, imperfections and all.

Handmade quilts were some of Sadie's favorite items that were brought into the shop. Whenever she received one, she loved looking it over carefully, in awe of the time, energy, and love that went into making each one. She imagined who may have curled up under it on a cold night, or what baby may have been swaddled in it to stay cozy.

The store had two large racks where the quilts hung, staggered so people could see them easily for purchase. One rack held quilts made by JoJo and the women in town, and the other rack had ones that came in with estate sales and other boxed items. Sadie couldn't imagine things so precious being tossed into a box to give away, but after working in the store most of her life, she also knew that it wasn't always easy for people to keep every family heirloom. Sometimes, things just had to be let go.

She loved picturing herself as the middleman. The person who would help get a special item from one family to the next. There was no guarantee that a new family would cherish something as much as the last, but she always hoped. Or maybe it was something that meant little to the person who brought it to her and would mean everything to the one who took it home.

The sound of someone humming took her from her thoughts. She looked toward the back door at Gary Wall, who was installing a new window. The door was open so he could move back and forth, working on both sides. Inspecting one side of the frame, he ran his fingers gently down the wood, now singing softly about no sunshine when she's gone. A tune Sadie had always liked, one that captured the fine balance between melancholy and acceptance.

"I give your aunt grief every day for not snagging that man." Moira came up beside Sadie and whispered in her ear. She shook her head. "I'll never understand." Taking a stack of invoices near Sadie, Moira turned and went back into the office.

Sadie smiled. She had to agree with Moira. Only a few years older than JoJo, Gary didn't look a day over fifty. The years had been good to him. Maybe it was time for Sadie to ask JoJo point blank why she'd never let herself fall for him.

"Excuse me, ma'am."

Lost in thought about her aunt, Sadie hadn't heard anyone come through the front, the bell above the door not even drawing her from her thoughts.

She turned to see a man standing on the other side of the counter from her, a young boy about the age of eight in front of him. The man's hands rested on the boy's shoulders.

"Hello, there." Sadie smiled. "I'm so sorry I didn't hear you come in. How may I help you?"

"My name is Albert, and my son here has something he'd like to tell you," The man said.

Sadie looked at the boy, who stared at the floor as if he wanted it to swallow him whole.

"Okay."

"I'm so sorry, ma'am. I broke your window." His voice was barely audible, his eyes still on the floor.

His dad squeezed his shoulders a bit.

The boy looked up at her, his eyes filled with fear as he fought back tears. "I'm so very sorry. I broke your window. My friends and I were playing baseball in the alley, and we…" He looked down again.

"I see," Sadie said as she nodded. A few days ago, she'd been irritated that no one had stepped up and admitted to breaking her window, but looking into this boy's eyes made her heart melt in her chest. He was close to the age she was when her mother left, and she'd lost her grandparents. The world could be a scary place for kid that young.

"Thank you for coming here to tell me," Sadie said. "That was a brave thing to do."

The boy looked up at her again, and she made sure to

smile at him. It wasn't hard to see he hadn't expected a friendly face on the receiving end of his apology.

"We talked in Sunday School about being honest," he said, then looked down.

"And he is more than willing to pay for the damages." Albert looked over at Gary working on the window then back to Sadie. "However, I would like for Kenny to pay for it himself and that's going to take a while as he saves up his allowance."

Sadie saw Kenny swallow hard at his dad's words. His allowance couldn't be much at that age, and he probably envisioned being broke until he was eighteen. She pursed her lips together to hold back a chuckle. This poor kid.

"I tell you what. How about we make a deal?"

The furrowed brow of both the boy and his father did make Sadie chuckle.

"How about you work off the debt?"

"I don't understand," the boy said.

"This is a big shop, and there is always something to dust or clean around here. If it's okay with your dad, how about you come by after school, say, two days a week for a month and help me here in the store for an hour or two and that will make us even."

Sadie could see Gary's grin out of the corner of her eye.

"Are you sure about that, ma'am?" Albert asked.

"I'm absolutely sure," Sadie said with a nod.

The boy looked around the store, his eyes wide as he

took it all in. "You'd trust me to do that?" he asked.

"I would."

"Even after I broke your window?" His eyes cast down once again.

"Well, the way I see it, Kenny. Kenny, right?" Sadie asked.

"Yes, ma'am," the boy nodded and looked at her.

"The way I see it is, we all make mistakes. And you owned up to yours, and you were honest with me. It's always good for us to face the consequences of our actions, and one way you can do that is to help me."

Kenny looked up at his dad. "Can I, Dad?"

"Yes, you may. I think Miss…" he looked at Sadie for help.

"Sadie. Sadie Woods." She stuck out her hand for them both to shake, which they did.

"I think Miss Woods is very kind and has a great idea for you to work off your debt."

The front door opened, the bell sound tinkling through the air. Sadie looked over to see James come through the door, a teenage girl right in front of him. With long hair the same shade as his and big blue eyes, it had to be his daughter, Maddie.

Not in his uniform, James had on worn jeans, a blue Henley shirt, and work boots. With a shadow of a beard and dark brown jacket, he had an outdoorsy vibe that every fiber in Sadie's being responded to, including her cheeks flushing.

Whether he noticed her blushing or not, the man across from her smiled and thanked her again. "We'll be going now, but Kenny will be here tomorrow after school if that works for you."

"It's perfect." She turned her attention to the boy. "And thank you again, Kenny, for coming to tell me you broke my window. That took a lot of guts."

"Excuse me." James made his way over to them as Maddie wandered toward the area of the store that held old books. "I couldn't help but overhear." He pulled a baseball from his jacket pocket. "I think this might belong to you." He held the ball out for the boy to see.

"It is! Thank you, mister!" Kenny said as he took the ball and looked at it as if he'd been handed a pot of gold he'd lost.

"James, this is Kenny and his dad, Albert. Albert and Kenny, this is James Larsen. He's our Deputy Sheriff and found the ball the other day."

Kenny shrunk back a little at this news, clutching the ball a bit closer to his chest.

"Kenny came to apologize, and we just agreed on a plan for him to work off his debt." Sadie smiled as she looked at Kenny and then James.

James reached out and shook Albert's hand and then did the same with Kenny. "It takes a big man to admit when he's wrong. Good for you, coming to Miss Sadie to tell her what happened. She's a nice lady. I'm sure you'll enjoy working for her." James turned his attention to Sadie and winked.

Before her brain could process the effect his attention had on her, Albert said, "Well, we better be going. Thank you again, Miss Sadie, for your grace and understanding."

"I'm glad to have met you both, and I will see you tomorrow." She pointed a finger at Kenny and smiled.

"Yes, ma'am." Kenny nodded as his dad led them out the front door.

Sadie and James watched them both go. Once the front door was closed, James turned to Sadie. "That was a nice surprise. He seems like a good kid."

"He does," Sadie agreed. "It took guts for him to come and apologize.

"Agreed. It was good timing for you to come in while they were here and give him his baseball back." Sadie wondered if there were any other reasons James stopped by, but she shooed those away from her thoughts.

"It was. I was actually coming to give it to you in case anyone showed up." James looked over his shoulder at Maddie, who now had her head buried in a book she'd found on the shelf.

"It's also my day off, and I picked up Maddie from school and wanted to spend some time with her."

Sadie smiled. "That's nice."

James put his hands in his pockets, his eyes cast down. "I don't get nearly as much time with her as I would like."

He rubbed the back of his neck with one hand, then put it back in his pocket. "But I do what I can."

It wasn't hard to see how much James loved his daughter. Sadie couldn't help but wonder if he carried more guilt than necessary, though, when it came to parenting.

"I don't have children of my own, but what I know from friends who do is that parenting is hard. One of the hardest things in life."

James looked at her. "That is the absolute truth."

Neither of them said it out loud, but Sadie sensed they were both thinking the same thing: James had to do it alone. It had been shocking news for the community when his wife had died, the local papers covering the story with vigor. James was a local hero to many, the Golden Boy who became an NFL star and now protected their town. However, other than knowing she'd driven her car into a tree, Sadie didn't pay attention to any other details of his wife's death. It wasn't as if she and Tiffany had been friends, and besides that, it wasn't any of her business. Based on the weight Sadie could see James carrying over being a single dad, she couldn't imagine the heaviness of grief he also carried over losing his wife.

Sadie turned her attention to Maddie. "Looks like she's quite a reader."

James looked at Maddie then back to Sadie, a smile on his face now. It was easy to see that the subject of her daughter lit him up from the inside out. "Reminds me of you when we were teenagers."

Sadie blinked then stared at him. Like her when they were teenagers? He didn't even know who she was when they were young. How did he...?

James chuckled. "I remember seeing you curled up in a chair while reading in the library. It was intimidating how smart you were. How smart you still are."

Sadie swallowed hard, her brain trying to catch up with all that he was saying. Not only did he know who she was, but he also noticed her then. Noticed her enough to recall all these years later her favorite chair in the library, her place of refuge when the hallways full of high school drama became too much.

Aware that her face was now flushed with heat, her cheeks probably red beacons giving away how topsy-turvy her insides were, she looked down and shuffled some papers around on the counter.

All these years, she'd thought he didn't even know her name.

James' smile wavered a bit. "I'm sorry if I made you uncomfortable."

Sadie shook her head and blinked her mind back to working order. "No, no," she waved her hands for a moment before folding them on the counter – the blessed counter that stood between them, holding her up. "I'm sorry. I just...I hadn't thought about the library or that chair for quite a while."

It felt like a decent save, but based on James' grin, he was aware there was more to her blushing than the thought of a chair. She needed to change the subject and do so immediately.

"It's wonderful that Maddie loves to read."

"It is." James agreed. "I don't have to battle her over being on her phone like some other parents of fifteen-year-olds I know, and for that, I'm grateful."

Sadie moved from around the counter. "I'd be happy to show her some of my favorites."

"That would be great. She will love that." James looked around. "I'll go say hello to Gary while you two talk books."

"Sounds good." Sadie made her way over to Maddie, if anything, grateful for a moment out of James' vicinity to catch her breath. Between the scent of his cologne, his blue eyes a swirl of emotions one moment and then teasing her the next, her heart rate was up, and her mind still trying to wrap around James Larsen paying any attention to her whatsoever – as a teen or now as a grown woman.

She shook her head and approached his daughter. "Hello, there."

Maddie looked up from the book in her hands. She tucked her hair behind her ear, which had fallen forward while she was reading. "Hello."

The girl's twinkling blue eyes and the warmth of her smile made her the spitting image of her dad. Sadie looked over at James who was now deep in conversation with Gary about the window, then back to Maddie.

"I'm Sadie Woods. I own this shop. And you're Maddie, yes?" Sadie stuck out her hand, and the girl shook it.

"Really? That is so cool. And yes, I'm Maddie. When my dad said we needed to go by the antique shop today after school, I thought that might be lame, but this place is amazing."

Sadie smiled.

"Sorry. No offense. It's not lame at all."

"None taken. I get it. Antiques aren't for everyone. For me, it's the history of it all that I love."

"I like history, too. Doesn't make me the coolest kid at school, but whatever…"

Sadie searched Maddie's face and her tone of voice for signs of sadness but found none. It was a statement of fact, not unlike how Sadie had felt in high school. She wasn't a cool kid and, quite frankly, was grateful. It always seemed so exhausting.

"What kinds of books do you like to read?"

"I like mysteries. And historical fiction."

"Me, too!"

Sadie stepped past Maddie to reach for a book on the shelf just behind where Maddie stood. "This is one of my favorites. It has history, romance, and a bit of mystery all rolled into one."

"That sounds awesome." Maddie took it and turned it in her hand to read the back of the book.

"Take it. Read it and let me know what you think."

"Really? I don't mind paying for it. I have babysitting money I can use to buy it."

Sadie put a hand on Maddie's arm. "No need. It's my gift to you, one history and mystery reading nut to another."

Maddie laughed and hugged Sadie. "Thank you so much."

Sadie's heart melted as she watched the girl take the book and sit down on the floor to explore it more. One of Sadie's favorite things was to sit on the ground, flipping through various books. She could do so for hours.

"What books are these?" Maddie asked, pointing at stacks on the floor near the shelves.

"Oh, well, those are ones I haven't gone through yet. Quite a bit of stuff gets brought into the store, and it takes time to go through it all. Of course, I know I take more time with books than anything else, so those are a never-ending project."

Maddie turned and moved to her knees so she could get a better look at the stacks. "These are so great. I would love to help you go through them."

"Really?" Sadie tucked her hands into the back pocket of her jeans. "I'm afraid I can't pay you though."

"That's okay. I have all half days of school next week leading up to Homecoming. It would give me something fun to do."

Sadie smiled. "Sounds good, but only if it's okay with

your dad."

"If what's okay with her dad?" James asked. He'd come up behind Sadie, the timbre of his voice and warmth behind her sending a tingly wave through her system.

Maddie looked up as Sadie turned to him. "I want to help Miss Woods go through these books. Can I, Dad?"

James looked at his daughter, then Sadie. "It's fine by me. It would have to be after school, of course."

Sadie looked up at James. He was close enough for her to wonder what it might be like for him to lean down and place a soft kiss on her lips.

"Sadie?"

She shook away the kissing fantasy and looked down at Maddie. "Of course. I would love the help."

Get a handle on yourself, Woods.

Oblivious to her struggle, James said, "That's settled then. Come on, Mads. We need to go. We have a few more errands to run."

"Yes, Dad." Maddie stood, the book Sadie gave her tucked close to her chest.

"What's that?" James asked.

"Miss Woods gave it to me." Maddie held it close as if it were a precious treasure.

"Sadie, please."

Maddie nodded. "It was nice to meet you, Sadie. And thank you again for the book."

Maddie stepped past them and headed toward the front

door.

James pointed a thumb over his shoulder. "We need to go, but we'll be seeing you soon, I guess. With Maddie helping you…"

"Yes. Sounds good. See you soon."

James turned to leave but then stopped. With a turn of his head, he said, "It was good to see you, Sadie." And with another wink, he was out the door and gone.

6

THE NEXT DAY, James sat in his squad car, parked outside of Get and Gather. He'd gone into the store the day before with Maddie to return the baseball but hadn't anticipated the depth of his attraction to Sadie. There may have been some truth to his brother's remarks about James having a little bit of a crush on her in high school, but they were now both adults. A crush was far from what he was feeling.

He noticed every little thing about her, from how she blinked at him when he said something that threw her off guard to how her hair smelled like lavender, which made him think of springtime, full of hope and warmth. Just like Sadie. And he would put money on the fact that as she'd looked up at him right before he left the store, she wanted him to kiss her as much as he wanted to oblige.

And there was no end to her kindness and how she treated people. If it were his window that had been broken, he wasn't sure he'd be as accommodating as she was about the whole thing. It was a stroke of thoughtful genius to give the boy a job after school to work off the broken window.

He ran a hand through his hair and gripped the steering wheel. She also had the uncanny ability to disarm him and his feelings. Not one to share much about…anything, he'd said to her more in a five-minute conversation than he had to anyone besides his brother in years. Sure, admitting he wanted more time with Maddie wasn't some deep, emotional secret, but one look into those eyes of hers and Sadie had him wanting to tell her anything she wanted to know.

James had told Mark the truth. The thought of dating terrified him. And yet, every time he was around Sadie, he relaxed. When he wasn't around her, he found himself eager to see her again, even coming up with reasons to do so.

Which was why he was sitting in his car, staring at the front door of her shop.

Maddie was beyond excited Sadie had asked her to help go through books at the shop. It was killing her that she had to wait to do so, but with after-school activities and projects, the following week was best. The school always gave the kids half days during the week that led up to Homecoming so they could work on class floats. Nearlake treated Homecoming like a major holiday, a holiday James would be happy to skip.

However, during dinner the night before, Maddie told him that Sadie said she couldn't afford to pay her. James had no problem with his daughter doing work for the sake of helping another person. What tugged at him was the reason behind it. Was Sadie in financial trouble? The morning he'd come by to check out the broken window, she seemed to have more on her mind than just the repairs.

He rubbed his chin and then opened his car door. If he sat there any longer, he risked having Sadie see him staring at her shop like an idiot. How would he explain that? He'd come up with a reason to stop by again, but not to sit out front and loiter.

The first thing James noticed as he walked through the front door was that the back window was fixed. It gave him peace of mind to know the back door was secure again, and he'd put money on the fact that it was done so quickly because Gary had a personal interest in the shop. Well, not the shop, but rather Sadie's aunt. Much like Sadie, JoJo Woods was a well-known member of the community, volunteering and popping up as often as her niece. James didn't know too much about her cancer diagnosis, but based on how Sadie seemed to carry the weight of the world on her shoulders, it couldn't be easy for them right now.

A young couple wandered an area of the store that held baby items, the woman's hand resting on her baby bump as she smiled at a pink blanket her husband held up for her to see. Another couple was on the other side of the store talking to Moira about children's toys and from what James could hear were wanting to find a gift for their grandson. Something that reminded them of when they were young.

James scanned the room and found Sadie. She stood in front of two tall wooden pieces that looked like wide ladders with folded quilts hanging from the rungs. A woman was admiring one. Based on their conversation, they knew one another. James wasn't surprised. Wherever he went in town, Sadie's name was mentioned as if she were old friends with everyone who lived in Nearlake.

Seeing that she was busy, James wandered the store. He had taken in a lot of it the day he'd been called in for the broken window, but now he saw it through different eyes. Before, he'd had his mind on theft and Sadie potentially being in danger. Now, he found himself drawn to a large oak wardrobe—the craftsmanship noticeable from halfway across the room. He made his way over to it, wanting to get a closer look.

He ran a hand over the front. The design on the door was etched by hand, something hardly seen in new furniture. Most things were factory made, many of them delivered in pieces to your door with the expectation of hours of frustration putting them together yourself.

"It's a beautiful piece, isn't it?"

Sadie's voice was like a ray of sunshine, warm against his back. He turned to look at her. Her hair color reminded him of fresh honey when the sunlight hit it. She had it pulled up into a ponytail, her brown eyes bright, and her hands tucked into the back pocket of her jeans. Another trait he'd noticed about her. She'd done the same thing when talking to Maddie.

Their eyes locked, and he couldn't look away. If he thought his attraction to her yesterday was something to think about, how he felt at that moment might require serious therapy.

"Yes. Beautiful."

Her cheeks flushed with color, and she blinked. Taking a step, she moved beside him to the wardrobe. They may have lost eye contact, but she was now a bit closer than before, and the scent of lavender jumbled his thoughts.

"I found it at an estate sale just a few weeks ago. The woman who sold it to me said it had been in her family for generations."

James forced himself to move his attention to the wardrobe. "It's easy to see a lot of time and skill went into making it."

"Do you know about woodworking?" Sadie asked. She looked up at him now, her face less flushed than moments ago.

"I do." James stuck his hands in the pockets of his uniform jacket. "It's a bit of a hobby," he said with a shrug.

What was it about this woman that turned him into a shy teenager? He was struggling to find words and when he did find them, they felt weird in his mouth and awkward to say.

"That's wonderful." Sadie opened the doors of the wardrobe so they could see inside. "I'm in awe of anyone who can create something like this. Being the reader I am, wardrobes always make me think of Narnia and wonder if there's another world inside of it somewhere." She leaned in and ran a hand over the back of the wardrobe.

"I can't say I've ever made anything quite like this."

"What kinds of things do you like to make?" She asked as she backed out of the wardrobe and faced him.

Her eyes searched his for an answer, the sincerity behind them causing him to relax. Feel more like a grown man again.

"Well, Maddie is into the HGTV shows, so we watch them a lot. So I tend to do more renovations on our house than build things."

"That's building things. It's a skill I'm jealous of, quite frankly. JoJo and I have some projects around our house, and I would love to know how to fix them myself."

"I'd be happy to teach you. Or even help with anything you need done at your place."

She crossed her arms in front of her and said, "Oh, no. I couldn't ask you to do that." As she looked down at her feet, she said, "It would be best for me to know how to do it myself."

James felt a twist in his gut at her response. Something

in her tone told him she didn't want to admit she couldn't pay him, and it wasn't his intention anyway. He'd offered as a friend. It reminded him of why he'd come into the store, however.

"I understand," he said. "I would be happy to show you a few things if you'd like, and the offer is open ended if you need some help, one friend to another."

She smiled at him and nodded.

"So, what brings you by today?" she asked.

"I was looking for something for Maddie. I wanted to maybe buy a couple more books for her, but she's also been wanting a more grown-up dresser. The one she has we bought when she was little and she's at that age where she wants her room to be more grown up. Although I don't know how a bright blue fuzzy bean bag in one corner and posters of favorite musicians say grown up."

Sadie laughed. "Ah, the contrary nature of teenage girls."

James nodded.

"I think I may have just the thing for you." She waved a hand, motioning for him to follow as she turned and wandered through the store.

He watched as she navigated her way around side tables and large tufted chairs, her hand at one point reaching out to glide along the wood of a console table. It was as if she wanted to be connected to all of it.

They worked their way through the main part of the

store and then through an archway that led to another large room. In the corner was a doorway that, from what James could tell, was an office. Sadie wandered through yet another archway into a room that was smaller yet still filled with furniture, trinkets, and Christmas ornaments – pretty much anything he could think of could be found.

"This is like a labyrinth of treasure," he said.

The smile on Sadie's face when she turned to him lit up the room. "I'm so glad you see it that way. Many people see it as junk, like some sort of glamourized garage sale." Her smile faded a bit as she picked up a folded piece of lace that was nearby on an end table and ran a hand over it. "But I see all of it as history. History that has been made and history yet to *be* made with whoever takes an item home."

"That's a romantic way to see it."

She looked at the lace again and said, "I guess it is. Someone might see this as just a piece of old lace when it was actually hand-woven at a shop in Burano, Italy. The woman running the estate sale where I bought it said it was found with a photo of the owner on a trip to Italy in 1957. On the back of the picture, she had written about her day trip to Burano and what drew her to the beauty of the lace, not to mention her awe of it being handmade."

Sadie tenderly set the lace back down.

"There really is history in each of these items."

"There is."

"You seem to know a lot about all of this," James

looked around.

"I've worked in this store for as long as I can remember. My grandparents were the original owners, then my aunt, and now me. Well, it's not mine yet, officially. But it will be." A shadow dimmed her eyes as her smile faded.

James tucked his hands into the pockets of his jacket. "How is your aunt doing?"

"Better," Sadie said with a small, somewhat forced smile. "Radiation has been tough, but the doctors are optimistic."

"That sounds good."

James had lost Tiffany in an accident. Quick. No warning. That was bad enough. He couldn't fathom losing a loved one slowly, watching them struggle and suffer along the way. The more he got to know about Sadie, the more he understood the heaviness he'd seen when the back window was broken. And he wanted to do anything he could to help.

Sadie pointed to the corner of the room. "Over here is the piece I think Maddie might like."

More tall and narrow than wide and low, the dresser was a mix of a greenish blue and grey with five drawers, each one with a golden swirl design that gave the piece a 1920s Gatsby vibe. The handles were vertical gold rectangles, and the feet were gold as well.

"This is really cool," James said as he ran a hand over the top. "All I said was Maddie's bean bag chair was blue, and yet this would practically match it."

"It is cool, isn't it? I know I only met her briefly, but I had a sense this would be something Maddie might like. I know I love it."

James smiled at her. "It sounds like it's tough for you to part with a lot of things in here."

She laughed at that, a sound that warmed his heart. "That is very true. I try not to get too attached, but there are definitely more things in here I'd like to keep than I would have space for at home." She shrugged. "And besides, each piece is meant for someone. Not just me."

"Like this one is meant for Maddie," he said, looking back at the dresser. "It really is perfect. I'll take it."

"I'm so glad. I know it will be in the right place with Maddie." She pointed a thumb over her shoulder and said, "You said you also wanted to look at some books?"

"I do." He put out a hand. "After you. I fear I'd get lost if I don't follow you anyway."

She laughed again as she turned to lead them back to the front of the store. They reached the same shelves Maddie had looked through the day before, and Sadie chose a few she thought Maddie would like.

James made his way to the counter to pay, the books for Maddie in hand.

"When can I swing by and get the dresser?" he asked. "It will need to be next week if that's okay. I took the week off to have some time with Maddie since she has half days. And I would need to grab my truck. I'm afraid the dresser won't fit in the back of my squad car."

"That's very true," Sadie said with a smile as she rang up his order. "Any time is fine. We also deliver."

James couldn't imagine how she had the time to run the store, take care of her aunt, volunteer all over town, *and* deliver furniture to people. The woman must never sleep.

He handed her his credit card. "Not a problem. I'm happy to come and get it."

Sadie rang the charge and handed back his card. "It's a date, then."

Their eyes met, and her cheeks flushed crimson.

"I mean…whatever date you want to come pick it up. We're here…whenever," she began gathering receipts and piling papers, anything to avoid looking at him.

"Thank you, Sadie." James waited until she looked at him again before he said, "It's a date."

With a wink, he turned and left.

7

SADIE FELT AS if she'd blinked, and it was Tuesday again. And not just any Tuesday, the Tuesday of Homecoming week. Nearlake put as much time and energy into the event as it did Christmas, and that was saying something. Christmas in Nearlake was downright magical.

Although she didn't play sports in high school, she did enjoy watching them. And the Homecoming game was a lot of fun. As odd as it could be at times to be back at your high school years after graduating, she enjoyed the school spirit and the community support.

Monday being the one day the shop was closed, Sadie had spent the afternoon making cupcakes for the bake sale the school library was holding to raise money for more books. JoJo had been able to help for a little while, but then spent the rest of the afternoon resting in her chair, chatting with Sadie as she'd decorated each cupcake in the school colors of green and gold.

Tuesday morning had flown by, a steady stream of customers coming into the shop. Another reason Sadie liked Homecoming Week was that it brought in more business. Rather than just come for the weekend, many alumni would arrive early and stay for the week, enjoying time with friends and family before the big game on Friday night.

As Sadie was finishing her lunch at her desk, Moira stuck her head in the door of the office. "Hey, there. Your young charges have arrived."

Sadie scrunched up her face. "Young charges?"

Moira smiled. "You know, the young man who broke the window and the hunky police officer's daughter you said could organize books."

Sadie shook her head at Moira calling James "hunky," whether that was true or not.

"It was a stroke of genius, if you ask me, to have his daughter hang out here after school. Get to know her, and have him hang around more. Good thinking, Sadie girl," Moira said with a click of her tongue.

It took every ounce of self-control Sadie had to not roll her eyes into the back of her head. "Moira. There was no hidden motive in asking Maddie or Kenny to be here after school. Kenny is paying off his debt with work, and Maddie *asked* if she could help organize the books. That wasn't even my idea."

"Whatever you say. Still can't hurt your cause though." Moira gave her a thumbs up then left.

"There's no cause!" Sadie yelled, but Moira was already gone.

It was beginning to feel as if every single person in her life was determined to set her up with James. However, she had wondered about how often she'd seen him since he'd answered her call about the broken window. She'd gone from seeing him around town, mostly at a distance, to having him in her shop three different times in one week's time.

Which wasn't entirely strange. The first time was because he was investigating the broken window. The second time, he'd come to return the baseball he'd found, and the third, to buy furniture for Maddie. But she had to admit that a part of her wondered, maybe even dared to hope, that he was stopping into the store to see her.

No. That couldn't be it. She was creating stories in her head. Ones that she had no time for. With all she had on her plate, love and romance would not fit. With a sigh, she sat back in her chair. It had been a long time since she'd considered anything resembling love in her thoughts, let alone her life.

Yet, when she was honest with herself, she had to admit she'd been thinking about James. A lot. The way his eyes lit up when he talked about Maddie. Or what a great listener he was. He had seemed truly interested when Sadie talked about the store, what it meant to her, and how she felt about the items that came through the door. Sincere and genuine were words that came to mind when she thought of him. And he was thoughtful, too. She knew he'd meant it when he offered to help her fix things around her house or even teach her to do it herself. And even though the thought of James as her own personal handyman brought about certain fantasies she dared not entertain, the last thing she wanted was to take up any of his time teaching her how to wield a hammer or working on her house when she had absolutely no means to pay him.

He'd been the star of their high school days, a spotlight seeming to follow him wherever he went, but she could see a shy, quiet side to him, one that made her think a lot of his demeanor back then had more to do with what was expected of him rather than his true self.

She chuckled. Wasn't that the definition of teen years right there? She doubted many people could honestly say that in those years, they were completely and totally themselves.

And now his daughter *was* in the store, as Moira had said, but not so Sadie could spend more time with James. She would never use Maddie as some pawn to get closer to him. Moira didn't mean that Sadie knew, but…ugh! Her thoughts were all jumbled since he'd showed up at her door a mere handful of days ago.

She stood up from her chair and swept the trash from lunch into the garbage beside the desk. With a brush of her hands over the bin, she tossed her thoughts in there as well. It was time to run her store and leave behind thoughts of dating, love, romance, and anything that had to do with James Larsen.

She made her way to the front of the store, where she found Moira showing Kenny how to dust shelves and Maddie at the counter holding a small metal storage box with daisies painted on the top. She looked up when she saw Sadie and smiled, her expression the spitting image of her dad's. There went the ability to forget all the things that had to do with James Larsen. Sadie would be spending the week staring into the face of a girl who had the same twinkle in her eye that he did.

Sadie was doomed.

"This is so cute," Maddie said as she popped the box open and looked inside. "It's so small, though. What's it meant to hold?"

Sadie stood on the other side of the counter, facing Maddie. "It's a pill box. Women used to carry them in their handbags."

Maddie looked at her. "What's a handbag?"

Goodness. Was Sadie that old? She didn't normally feel it, but at that moment, she feared a few gray hairs may have shown up.

"It's a purse."

Maddie nodded. "Oh. Right."

Sadie noticed then that like the other teenagers in town, Maddie didn't have a purse over her shoulder. Or a bag of any kind. It was probably safe to assume Maddie had a phone case that kids used that held ID and a credit card, all they could need or want fitting nicely in the back pocket of their jeans.

Handbags had been somewhat of an obsession for Sadie's grandmother. Owning an

antique shop could do that to a person. Some beautiful bags came through the store, some handmade pieces, and even some high-end designer ones. Sadie couldn't fathom paying full price for brand new.

The current generation seemed to have a less-is-more kind of mindset, not wanting to be bogged down with stuff, but where Sadie could see the convenience of a person's whole world being on their phone, she still didn't trust electronics to not give out, therefore leaving her stranded. She was more than fine with her paper calendar and notebook tucked neatly into her tote-sized *handbag*. She bit back a laugh at the fact that one of those pill boxes was tucked in there as well.

Maybe she was getting old.

Vintage had a nicer ring to it.

Maddie closed the pill box and set it back down on the counter. "I brought you that book you loaned me. I really liked it."

Sadie hadn't noticed the book sitting on the counter until Maddie picked it up and handed it to her.

"Wow. You're a fast reader."

Maddie shrugged.

Sadie put out a hand and gently pushed the book back toward Maddie. "It wasn't a loan. It was a gift."

"Really? Wow. Thank you."

"My rule on books is that they are meant to be re-read or passed along. So, if you want to keep it on your shelf and read it again someday, do that. Or find someone else you think might like it and let them have it."

Maddie smiled as she tucked her hair behind her ear with one hand and looked down at the book she held in the other. "I like that. I'll make that my rule, too."

The bell over the front door jingled and a group of women entered the shop. Moira welcomed them as she went over to see how she could be of help.

"Miss Sadie."

Sadie turned to see Kenny holding a duster in one hand, a big smile on his face.

"Hi, Kenny."

She introduced him to Maddie, who gave him a small wave and a smile.

"Miss Sadie, thank you so much for letting me do this. This is so fun!"

Sadie and Maddie shared a quick glance at one another.

"If you think dusting is fun, Kenny, this store is going to be your amusement park," Sadie teased.

Maddie laughed at that as Kenny headed off to dust his next row of shelves.

"Come on, Maddie. I'll talk you through the book stacks."

Sadie showed Maddie the various books she had piled against a side wall of the store.

"So, the thing is, I tend to have shelves for these. The problem is when a customer wants to come and buy the shelves. I started setting the books here, thinking I'd find another place for them, and just haven't got to it."

Maddie was already kneeling before a stack. "Okay. I can go through them and arrange them by genre or color of book covers or however you want.

"The world is your oyster, Kid. You can organize them

however you want and either put them on shelves or use them as décor in various places around the store."

"Really?" Maddie looked up at her, eyes wide in disbelief that Sadie trusted her with such a task.

"Really, really. Have at it." She patted Maddie on the shoulder. "Just give me or Moira a shout if you need anything. We will be around the store."

Maddie was already looking back down at the books, her long blond hair flowing down her back and covering the sides of her face. It made Sadie smile and think of how often she had done the very same thing in her life. She could get lost in books for days.

She breathed in deep and let it out. Too bad those days seemed long gone. Now, they were filled with so much responsibility. Not that she was complaining. She loved her life. She did. But she wouldn't mind a day here and there with nothing but time to read.

She left Maddie to it and went to check on Kenny. Seeing him happily running the duster over any surface he could reach, she decided to tackle prepping the dresser James had bought for when he was ready to pick it up. She liked to wrap items as well as possible so there would be no damage in transport.

Between customers coming and going, keeping an eye on Kenny, answering the phone, and chatting with friends who were in town for Homecoming, the afternoon flew by. Sadie had yet to get to finish prepping the dresser and was back to working on it when Maddie joined her.

"Sadie. I think I found…" her shoes squeaked as she

stopped short on the wood floor. "What is that? Is that a dresser? No way. It is so cool!" She hurried over to it, running her hands along the top, her eyes wide, a huge grin on her face. "Oh, man. It has a Sold sign on it. What a huge bummer."

Sadie hated to see the girl's shoulders sag and her face fall. But, seeing Maddie's joyful reaction, Sadie didn't want to ruin the surprise for James when he told Maddie it was for her.

"Yep. It was sold recently." Although she hadn't lied, Sadie still avoided eye contact with Maddie, not wanting to give away anything with a smile or any kind of facial expression.

"Ugh. I want a new dresser so bad, and this would be perfect."

Wanting to draw Maddie's attention away from her disappointment, Sadie said, "When you came over to me, you said you had found something?"

"Oh yeah. Right." Maddie snapped her fingers. "You need to come and see."

Intrigued, Sadie followed Maddie back over to where the stacks of books had been. In a short time, Maddie had worked her way through quite a few. Sadie noticed a few books stacked on a console table nearby, a set of bookends shaped like monkeys holding them up. Another stack lay on its side on a nightstand, each book with a green cover matching the hue in the bed comforter folded nearby.

The girl had an eye for decorating. James mentioned watching HGTV shows with her, and Sadie could see proof of that.

Sadie looked where Maddie stood and saw a corner of one of the rugs pulled up, a square of wood cut out of the floor.

"Well, that's odd." She moved closer, her hands on her hips as she looked down.

Maddie knelt beside her. "I know, right? I dropped a book, and when it hit the floor, it made a hollow sound. I got down and knocked on the floor a bit, and when I moved back the rug, I found this."

"I've been in this shop since I was a kid, and I have never seen that."

"Maybe it's been hidden by the rug this whole time."

Sadie searched her memories, ones of days doing much of what Kenny was doing when she was about his age, moving through the store with wonder and curiosity, a duster leading the way. Nothing popped up about that spot, though. Nothing. Even during all the time, she'd run the store with JoJo. Maddie could very well be right, though. That rug could have easily been placed by Sadie's grandparents or JoJo, not as one for sale, but to cover the floors.

Sadie kneeled down next to Maddie and moved more of the rug back, revealing more of the floor.

"Wait. Is that…" she asked.

"It's a handle."

Tucked into the floor was a brass handle. Sadie lifted it and pulled. The square piece of floor creaked as it came up, turning on a small hinge.

"No. Way." Maddie looked down into the dark space

and then at Sadie. "I think we just found a secret passageway."

8

SADIE STARED DOWN into the blackness of the hole in the floor of her shop. Never once had she heard her grandparents talk about anything like this, and she certainly would remember if JoJo had.

"Oh my gosh, Sadie." Maddie stuck her head down closer to the opening. "This is just like out of the Nancy Drew story about the hidden staircase."

"Okay, Maddie, as much as I love that your mind goes straight to novels, I have no idea what this is. And I would imagine it isn't as exciting as a secret passageway beneath the store. It's probably some kind of cellar."

Even as she said the words, she couldn't keep her imagination from joining Maddie's. Sadie wanted to temper Maddie's eagerness a bit, though, even if her own mind, which also loved those kinds of books, couldn't help but wonder if they'd stumbled upon a great story of their own.

Maddie pulled her phone from her back pocket and turned on the flashlight. It didn't illuminate much, but it did reveal a wooden staircase.

"No. Way." Maddie said. "This is so amazing. There *is* a secret passageway! I so, totally want to go down there."

She shifted her body as if she was going to do that very thing when Sadie put a hand on her arm.

"Just hold on a second, Maddie. There is no way I am letting you do that."

The girl's shoulders sagged. "Come on, Sadie! This is incredible. I *have* to see what's down there."

Moira's idea that Sadie had asked Maddie to work in the shop to get closer to James came to Sadie's thoughts, as well as how fast James would sprint out of her life if she let his daughter anywhere near that black hole.

"Okay. Okay. Look. I'll admit I'm as curious about all of this as you are, but this is way too dangerous. For either of us. I'm not going down there either until I can figure out a way to do so where no one gets hurt."

"We can ask my dad!" Maddie said, her eyes brightening at the possibility.

"Let's not tell your dad about this just yet. I need to ask my aunt if she knows anything about it, and we can go from there."

Maddie's face fell. Sadie had forgotten what a roller

coaster teen emotions could be and how much they showed in voice and mannerisms. She felt as if she'd literally crushed Maddie's joy multiple times in a matter of minutes, and although she hated that, she wasn't about to back down. It was far from a good idea for anyone to go down there any time soon.

"Agreed?" She wanted confirmation before moving on.

Although it was clear Maddie was disappointed, Sadie had a feeling James had taught his daughter common sense, as well as it being best to listen to adults, so she believed her when Maddie nodded in agreement.

"Okay."

"Let's put this back the way it was. I don't need anyone tripping over the rug or anyone else finding the door and going down there without me knowing. Can you even imagine what would happen if Kenny found this?"

That made Maddie laugh. "True. It probably is best to keep this between us for now," Maddie said.

Relieved that Maddie wouldn't try to do anything reckless or share their discovery with anyone, Sadie closed the trapdoor and placed the rug back over it.

"I'll set some stacks of books there as well."

"Good idea." Sadie stood and brushed the dust off her jeans just as Maddie's phone rang.

"Hey, Dad," she said when she answered. She listened for a moment and then said, "I'm sure I can wait here until you're done or find a ride."

Sadie couldn't help but overhear the conversation. She tapped Maddie on the shoulder and pointed to herself as she whispered, "I can take you home if you need."

As she said it, an idea formed in her head. She could take the dresser as well. Deliver it for James so he wouldn't have to come and get it.

Maddie was still on her knees on the floor. She looked up at Sadie and nodded. "Actually, Sadie just said she can bring me home." A pause. "I'm sure it's fine, Dad, or she wouldn't have offered."

Sadie bit back a smile at James' protest, thoughtfully not wanting to take away any of Sadie's time. She whispered to Maddie, "I'm more than happy to do it."

"She just said she's more than happy to do it." Maddie smiled up at her. "Okay. See you later. Love you, too. Bye."

Maddie ended the call and put her phone back in her pocket. "He's worried he is inconveniencing you, but I told him it was fine."

"It is absolutely fine." Sadie's phone dinged with a text message. "I just need to finish wrapping the dresser to deliver it tonight. I'll get Ned to help us load it, and then we'll be off."

"Sounds good." Maddie turned her attention to the books and began again to sort the stacks.

Sadie looked at her phone as she headed back to the dresser.

It was a text from James.

Are you sure you're okay giving Maddie a ride home? I have some errands to run, and they are taking longer than anticipated. I thought my parents could drive her, but they can't.

Sadie smiled as she typed her response.

No problem. As she said, I wouldn't have offered if I didn't mean it.

She turned to be sure Maddie wasn't around to see what she typed next.

I was actually just going to text you and ask if I can deliver the dresser when I come. Maddie saw it and fell in love with it. I played dumb and didn't give away that it's for her. You can still surprise her with it.

That sounds perfect. Thanks again.

He ended his message with a smiley face emoji that made Sadie giggle. A man not afraid to use emojis. He did have a teenage daughter, which might explain that, but still. It had Sadie giggling like a teenager as well, something bubbling up inside her that she hadn't felt in a really long time.

Joy.

* * *

It didn't take too long for Sadie to get the dresser wrapped up and her employee and friend, Ned, helped her load it. With the delivery tied tight into the back of Sadie's truck and with Maddie in the passenger seat, they were on their way to James and Maddie's house.

True to her word, Maddie hadn't mentioned the trapdoor again, certainly not in front of Moira or Kenny, or anyone at the shop. But there was a new energy buzzing from the young woman. Sadie had to admit she felt the same kind of vibration. Although she wasn't sure it was entirely from them finding a secret door in the floor of her shop. More of it was from knowing she was about to see James again. And she'd be lying if she said she wasn't more than curious about what his house looked like.

James had been a wide receiver in the NFL. It wouldn't be surprising if he had a mansion somewhere outside of town.

"Turn here," Maddie said. She'd been guiding Sadie on the drive.

As Sadie turned into the driveway, she found herself chuckling inside. The house was gorgeous and, not surprisingly, settled on the edge of the lake, but it was far from what most people would expect. A beautiful ranch-style craftsman house, but not a mansion. Sadie couldn't help but notice that the lights on inside glowed as the sun made its way down in the sky, not unlike her windows, which beckoned her home every evening.

"You can park around back," Maddie said.

"Okay." Sadie followed the driveway that curved around the side of the house and led to a large concrete area for parking. A workshop with the same design and color as the house was behind it, not far from where a small dock sat in the lake, and two yellow Adirondack chairs side-by-side on the shore before it.

Two black labs lay in the grass not far from the dock. Their ears perked up when they saw Sadie's truck, but the second they eyed Maddie as she got out, their faces lit up with doggie joy, and they trotted toward her.

Sadie got out of the truck and shut the door.

"Hey, puppies. How are my dogs?" Maddie said as she rubbed their ears. The dogs spun around, happily receiving the love their owner gave.

"This is Chip and Joanna," Maddie said, each dog's ears perking up at the sound of their names.

Sadie chuckled. "Your dad said you were an HGTV fan."

"I am. Fixer Upper is my favorite."

The door of the workshop opened, and James stepped out. Sadie had to fight back an audible sigh, not to mention the handyman fantasy again. What was it about a man in jeans, a t-shirt, and work boots? It didn't hurt that his jeans fit him perfectly in all the right places, and his shirt looked as if it had been tailored for the muscles in his chest and arms. His hair was a bit mussed as if he'd run his hands through it while working. He looked as if he hadn't shaved in a day or two, the short beard a look Sadie liked very much.

Sadie shook her head. It was not the time to let her thoughts go any further down that path. The man's daughter was right there.

"Hey, Dad."

"Hey, Mads."

He was rubbing his hands on a cloth that he then tucked into the back pocket of his jeans.

"It's good to see you, Sadie," he said, his tone sending a shiver through Sadie as if he'd touched her.

"You, too." She moved toward the back of the truck if anything to give herself something to do besides ogle the man or think of how just his voice made her all upside down and sideways.

"Thanks for giving Maddie a ride home," he said as he made his way over to them. "That was thoughtful of you."

"No problem."

"You should see this dresser, Dad. It's amazing. Sadie said she needs to deliver it tonight," Maddie said as she walked over to her dad. The dogs followed and sat beside her.

"She just did." James smiled at his daughter.

Maddie's face went from looking confused to realizing what her dad meant. She launched herself at him, wrapping her arms around him in a huge hug. "No way! Dad! This is amazing. You got this for me?"

James held his daughter, one hand cradling the back of her head. Sadie could imagine him holding Maddie as a baby, those big strong arms promising to never let her go. An empty space in her heart ached as she watched them. She'd never known her father. What must that be like to feel so safe in the arms of a man who loved you so?

"I did. However, I have to say that Sadie chose it. She said she thought you would like it." He smiled at Sadie over his daughter's head.

"I don't just like it – I *love* it!" Maddie let go of her dad and jumped up and down with her hands clenched together. She squealed with delight and then went about helping them get the dresser out of the truck. They tucked it in the garage with promises from James that he and Maddie would move it into her room after dinner.

"I'm really glad you love the dresser, Maddie, and that we could get it to you today." Sadie lifted one hand in a little wave. "I guess I'll see you tomorrow afternoon."

She turned to go, but James stopped her.

"Sadie. It really was so nice of you to do this. Why don't you stay for dinner? I made Maddie's favorite, and there's more than enough to share."

"Aw, Dad. You did a store run and came home to cook?"

James grinned. "You caught me."

I don't want to intrude on your time," Sadie said. She was aware he'd taken the week off to have more time with Maddie. The last thing she wanted was to get in the way of that.

"It's no intrusion," James said just as Maddie said, "Please stay! I would love it."

Sadie's eyes met James'. One side of his mouth tilted up, his head nodding slightly as if to agree with his daughter.

She looked at her watch. JoJo would be expecting her home.

"Please stay, Sadie," Maddie begged once more.

"Let me just check in with my aunt."

"Yay!" Maddie spun on her heels and headed into the house, the dogs trotting after her.

"I believe she took that as a yes," James said, a smile on his face.

"I believe so."

"She doesn't like to take no for an answer."

Sadie smiled. "I can see that. Just let me text JoJo and make sure she's okay."

James nodded. "I understand."

Sadie sent a quick message to her aunt, who responded right away with an all-caps answer of *ABSOLUTELY STAY AND HAVE DINNER! I AM FINE.* A line of winking smiley face emojis followed.

Sadie laughed.

"I'm guessing that means she is good?" James asked.

"Well, based on the amount of emojis, yes."

"Ah, yes."

"In fact, I noticed you sent an emoji in our text thread earlier," Sadie teased.

James lifted an eyebrow. "And?"

"I just didn't see you as an emoji-using kind of guy."

That got a full, deep laugh out of him, one that warmed Sadie's insides.

Their eyes met, and he said, "And just what kind of guy do you see me as?"

Kind. Thoughtful. Great father. A list of things popped into Sadie's head. She just couldn't seem to get them to come out of her mouth.

She looked away, her eyes drawn to a wooden rocking chair in the corner of the garage.

"What is that?" she asked as she made her way over to it.

James followed her.

"Did you make this?" She ran a hand over the arm of the chair, the wood smooth and perfect. "This is incredible."

She looked at James, who simply shrugged.

Although it was brand new, it had an antique vibe to it, the design similar to something made in the early 1900s.

"I know it's old school, but I like that. I wanted to make another one and put them both on the front porch." He tucked his hands into the front pockets of his jeans.

"One for you and one for Maddie."

James' mouth formed a small smile, but it didn't reach his eyes. Sadie sensed she was missing something about the chairs but didn't pry.

"It's perfect. Such a beautiful piece. And you said you weren't a craftsman," she teased.

He did smile at that. "One chair does not a craftsman

make."

"Ah, but you said you were going to make another one."

He laughed. "I did say that, yes."

The garage door opened. Maddie's head popped through it. "Are we gonna eat soon or what?"

"On our way," James answered. He looked at Sadie. "Shall we?"

She nodded. "Lead the way."

9

JAMES LED SADIE into the house. It would have made a
better impression had they gone through the front door
rather than the garage, but Sadie didn't seem to mind. Her
compliments began to flow right away.

"I love this mud room. We have one, too, and I love
that most of the homes in this area have them. They're such
a warm welcome after a long day, don't you think?"

James hadn't thought about the mud room at all other
than it was the place where he tripped over the shoes Maddie
kicked off after she came through the door. But seeing it
through Sadie's eyes, he could get a feel for what she was
talking about. Painted a light yellow it did give a sense of
warmth.

"Maddie chose the paint color. She chose all the colors,

come to think of it," he said as they made their way into the kitchen that was just off the mud room.

A few years back, James had begun to see Tiffany's handprint throughout the house still lingered. Maddie had only been ten when Tiffany died, so he hadn't wanted to change too much too quickly, but once Maddie began to have a strong interest in home design and décor, he told her she could come to him with any changes she wanted to make, and they would decide what was best and then do it together. Paint colors were the first thing. Initially, he'd been a bit nervous about having a teenage girl choose the colors for the house, but Maddie had a great eye and found neutrals with yellow, green, and brown tones that brightened up the place. Her mother had been drawn to darker, more dramatic tones, although Tiffany hadn't been thrilled to be back in Nearlake anyway and didn't find a house under 6,000 square feet worth fussing about.

The kitchen sat in the back of the house, large French doors opening from it out to a patio that looked over the lake. A small path led to the dock. The property was surrounded by huge fir trees, something James appreciated. It gave him a sense that they were tucked into their own private space, something he'd longed for during his years in the NFL. Something he was grateful he could give Maddie.

"Oh, my goodness," Sadie said as she entered the kitchen. "This is breathtaking." She moved through the room, her hand running along the white granite of the large island in the center of the kitchen.

Maddie had music playing, a country station with a song about a guy wondering how his evening would play out with a woman he was interested in. James glanced at Sadie.

He could relate.

The scent of cooked lasagna filled the air, causing his stomach to growl.

Maddie set down a pan of lasagna on a hot pad on the counter, her hands tucked into bright red potholders. "This is my grandma's recipe and my all-time favorite." She took the potholders off her hands and set them down. A large salad bowl rested nearby. She poured dressing over the lettuce and vegetables and then tossed it all together with wooden salad tongs.

Sadie looked at James. "You cook, too?"

"Just this one dish," he said, both hands held up.

"It's true," Maddie agreed. "Grandma taught him this one, but beyond that, he's hopeless."

"Hopeless feels like a bit of a stretch," James argued. "I make a pretty good hamburger."

Maddie stopped tossing the salad and looked as if she was thinking hard. "I'll give you that. But that's grilling. That's not full-on cooking."

James shook his head. He and Maddie could debate for days what was considered "real" cooking and what wasn't, but he wasn't going to drag Sadie into that. His head was still trying to wrap around the fact that she was here and had said yes to having dinner with them. A far cry from a date, but he was finding that he wanted any kind of time with her, and he would take what he could get.

He'd set the table for two but noticed another place setting. Maddie must have done that while they were still in the garage talking. It didn't escape him that he had asked Sadie what kind of guy she thought he was, and she avoided the question by diverting their attention to the rocking chair.

Which was fine. Seeing her cheeks flush when he'd asked was enough for him. He'd rattled her in a good way. And although painfully curious about what her answer might have been, he was a patient man. He'd find out soon enough what she thought of him and, hopefully, that she was thinking *of* him as often as he was thinking about her.

Yet again, she'd thrown him off as well, stirring up feelings he hadn't paid much attention to in recent years. He'd originally built the rocking chair with the goal of having two chairs, one for him and one for Tiffany. When he'd finished the chair and shown it to her, he'd said he made it as a symbol of being with her forever, growing old together and rocking on the front porch as they watched kids and grandkids play in the yard.

She hadn't found the idea quite as romantic as he had. Although she had said the chair was "cute" and having a couple on the porch would fit the motif of the house, she didn't like thinking about getting old or being a grandmother.

That had been their last conversation about it. James

put the chair in the garage, losing all motivation to build a second one.

Until now.

When Sadie had said he could build two for him and Maddie, it sounded nice, but Sadie was the one he could picture sitting there with him. A thought that brought both peace and turmoil to his gut. James had let himself think about what his brother had mentioned, that having a woman in his life could bring a lot of good. And it wasn't tough to imagine that with Sadie around. A lot about that felt peaceful. The turmoil part came when he thought of all that could go wrong. His heart had been stomped on and left in the dust. Was he ready to risk trusting it to someone again? And anyone who came into his life also came into Maddie's life. He had to consider that.

However, watching Sadie and Maddie talk about books and the dogs and HGTV as Maddie cut the lasagna and placed squares on plates, it wasn't hard to see that Maddie might like the idea of having Sadie around just as much as he did.

They settled into seats at the table, the dogs resting on their beds in the family room. Maddie continued her conversation with Sadie, and as they did so, their voices mixed with the music in the background, causing a sense of peace to settle over James. As much as he enjoyed time with his daughter, it was nice to have another person with them to share a meal. And not just any person.

Sadie.

His brother's idea of a nice candlelit dinner popped into James' head. It was not a vision he wanted to entertain when Mark first mentioned it, but it now sounded like something he'd like very much. A date with Sadie was sounding less and less intimidating.

He cut a piece of lasagna with his fork and brought it to his mouth. Every time he ate this meal, he thanked his mother for teaching him how to make it. The combination of flavors danced across his tongue. The tomato sauce rich with basil and oregano, the cheeses gooey and melted mixed in with the perfectly cooked noodles. He may not be able to make much else, but he could live the rest of his life off just this meal and be fine.

"Oh, my goodness. This is fantastic," Sadie said after finishing her first bite.

"Grandma does it better, but Dad's is a pretty good second," Maddie said, then dished a bite into her mouth.

James made a face. "Thanks, kid. Way to burst my bubble."

Maddie shrugged. "I'm just being honest. But Grandma should be the one that makes it best. It's her recipe."

James conceded with a shrug and took another bite.

"Well, I haven't tasted your grandmother's version, but I think this one is pretty amazing." Sadie smiled at him as she dished more into her mouth.

The compliment was just what James needed to put air

into his cooking confidence again. Not to mention, he felt as if the prettiest girl at school had just told him he was awesome.

"Thank you." He smiled at Sadie and turned his attention to his daughter, who was happily cutting her lasagna into perfect bite-sized squares. She'd done it since the first time he'd made her this meal. "How was book organizing at the shop today?"

"It was so fun," Maddie said as she put down her knife and fork. Easier for her to wave her hands around as she talked. "You would not believe some of the books that are in those stacks, Dad. One was published in 1898. No joke."

"I think there is one even older than that," Sadie said.

James couldn't help but notice the big smile on Sadie's face as Maddie talked. He'd been right that they were similar. Not just about books but history, too. A pang of regret hit him as he thought about their teenage years. All that time, he noticed her at school but never had the guts to talk to her. It sounded as silly in his head now as it was back then, him not being brave enough to befriend her. Unfortunately, the truth was that he was an idiotic kid who feared what would happen to his status at school if he had. He'd tried to be nice to everyone and make sure he wasn't a total jerk to anybody. But he stayed tucked into his own crowd, Tiffany included, and sitting here with Sadie across the table from him, her presence alone bringing him a sense of contentment he hadn't had in a long time – maybe ever—made his regret that much stronger.

"Maddie was a great help today. The collection of books is no joke. And she did a beautiful job finding places for them around the shop. She has a good eye for decorating," Sadie said as she smiled at James and then Maddie.

Maddie's face beamed from the compliment.

"And Kenny was there today," Sadie said as she laid her fork down and leaned back in her chair.

"Kenny?" James asked.

"The boy who broke my window," Sadie reminded him.

"Right." James nodded.

"He was quite excited about Moira teaching him how to use the feather duster," Sadie said with a laugh, the sound like music to James' soul.

"He totally was," Maddie agreed. "We just have to be sure he doesn't dust near the books or the secret passage…" She stopped as her eyes met with Sadie's.

James wasn't entirely sure, but he could swear that Sadie had nudged Maddie under the table with her foot.

Maddie's face went red. "Sadie, I am *so* sorry. Honestly. I didn't mean to say anything."

She covered her mouth with her fingers.

Sadie's eyes grew wide as she stared at Maddie.

James put down his fork and leaned forward. It didn't take the cop in him to know that something was going on between the two of them.

"Did you just say a secret passageway?" He looked at

his daughter but could see Sadie out of the corner of his eye. "And you avoiding eye contact, Sadie, makes you look just as guilty, so I'll get to you in a second," he said with a finger pointed at her but his eyes never leaving Maddie's.

Maddie looked at Sadie and then back at James.

"Spill it, kid." He was grateful when Sadie nodded in agreement.

"Sadie and I found a trapdoor in her shop. Well, I found it, but we opened it, and I really wanted to go down there, but Sadie said no, that you would be super mad. And I know she's right. But then she didn't want me to tell anyone, and now I've gone and blown it and…"

When James asked her to spill it, he honestly thought he'd be met with hesitation. But Maddie's verbal vomit was more than enough information for him to work with.

Maddie had stopped to take a breath while Sadie rubbed her forehead and then folded her hands in her lap, awaiting his interrogation.

He turned his attention to Sadie. "Well, that's quite a story."

"I didn't mean for her to keep anything from you. I would never ask her to do that. I was just concerned that if Kenny or Moira or anyone else knew, *they* would go down there, and I have no idea what it is or…" she shook her head.

"Okay, okay. You said secret passageway." James' brain was still taking in all his daughter had said. It seemed best to work from the top and go from there.

"Yes! It's so totally exciting. Like something out of a mystery novel."

His daughter had switched from contrite to animated in about two seconds. He knew she now believed he was in on the secret, and therefore, the adventure would begin.

"We don't know for sure it's a secret passageway," Sadie offered.

"What else could it be?" Maddie asked. "It's a door hidden in the floor, and when we opened it, there was a staircase leading down underground."

James looked at Sadie. "Seriously?"

She shrugged. "That's all true."

"And neither of you went down there, right?" James' gut clenched at the thought of either of them being under a building and having it cave in or… God only knew what could be down there.

"Absolutely not," Sadie said.

"No," Maddie said, the disappointment in her voice evident.

James leaned back in his chair and took a deep breath. His appetite was now gone, his mind on all that his daughter and Sadie had just told him.

"I don't remember my grandparents saying anything about it, but I will talk to JoJo as soon as I can to see if she knows anything," Sadie offered. "But until then, I want to keep this among us."

"But then, can we go down there?" Maddie asked.

Sadie wisely avoided the question. "There's a lot of history to that building. It was built in the early 1900s and was originally the site for the local newspaper. Almost all of the buildings along Lakeside Drive are original. My grandparents became tenants in the 1960s, but I have never heard anyone talk about anything under the shop."

James could tell Sadie was trying to be cautious about the whole situation but was just as curious as his daughter about what this possible secret passageway might be.

He had to admit his curiosity was piqued as well. It wasn't shocking to have a cellar beneath a structure like that, but the last thing he wanted was his daughter or Sadie crawling down there and getting hurt because they thought they were living in some adventure story.

"No one is going down here," he said.

Maddie frowned.

"At least not until I can see it and get a handle on what this actually is we are dealing with."

Maddie smiled again.

He shook his head. The teenage emotional roller coaster might be the death of him.

"Sadie will talk to her aunt and check the history of the building, but until then, no one even *looks* down that hole. Deal?"

They both said, "Deal," and nodded.

He believed them, but why did James feel like a

Pandora's box had just opened, and he had no idea what was inside?

10

SADIE RAN THE evening's events through her mind as she drove home.

After dinner, James and Maddie invited her to stay and sit by the lake for a bit around their fire pit. As much as she wanted to say yes to that, she was exhausted. And she didn't like leaving JoJo for so long in the evening.

Besides, the evening took an odd turn after Maddie spilled the beans about the trap door. Sadie shook her head as she turned into her drive. Was that really what they'd found? And if so, what in the world did it mean, if anything?

She turned off her truck and went inside the house.

"I'm home!"

"In here, Loves."

Sadie made her way into the living room and plopped

down on the sofa near her aunt's chair. JoJo was relaxed in her recliner, watching a movie on television. The remote was in her hand and she paused what she was watching. Her cheeks had good color and she looked more content than tired.

"Don't stop watching on my account," Sadie said.

"Oh, I have a feeling hearing about your date this evening is going to be way more interesting than anything I'm watching on TV."

Sadie had to laugh. If only JoJo knew. Actually, JoJo needed to know. She was the one person Sadie might be able to get answers from about the shop.

"It was not a date, Aunt Jo. Not even close. His daughter was with us."

JoJo shrugged as if that made no difference.

Sadie leaned against the arm of the sofa and curled her legs up beside her. She grabbed a throw pillow and hugged it to her chest. "It was a nice time. I gave his daughter, Maddie, a ride home from the store – I told you she's helping go through those books."

JoJo nodded. "You did. And God bless the girl for that. That's a big job."

"Agreed. Anyway, I took her home and delivered a dresser James had bought for her, and as a thank you, they asked me to join them for dinner. Simple as that."

"Hmmm."

"Don't hmmm me. It was."

"Continue," JoJo said. "I can tell you want to share more."

The memory of James coming out of the workshop came into her thoughts. He also stole glances at her all through dinner. And how he went into protective mode the minute he heard about the secret passageway. Rather than be bothered by his response, Sadie found it endearing to have him care about her welfare and his offer to help her figure it all out.

Leaving out any emotions or attraction she had toward James, Sadie chose to stick to the topic of the store.

"I do want to share more. Maddie found a trapdoor with stairs that lead down under the building. Do you know anything about that?"

JoJo shifted in her chair to sit up a bit. "Well, that's interesting. I'm sure I have no idea."

"Grandpa and Grandma never said anything to you?"

"Not a word." JoJo shook her head.

"Hmph." Sadie picked at a thread that hung off the throw pillow in her lap.

"Are you sure that's what it is? Some secret passageway?"

"No. Not really. But it is a trapdoor in the floor, and when we opened it, we could see a staircase that leads down into a dark cellar below."

"I'm assuming you were wise enough not to go down there."

Sadie shook her head. "No. We didn't. Maddie sure wanted to, though. She still wants to."

JoJo narrowed her eyes a bit, a small smirk on her lips. "And so do you."

Sadie lifted her eyes upward and pinched her mouth together. "Maaaayyybee……"

JoJo laughed. "Well, you should. So do I!"

Sadie held back a laugh thinking of how James would respond to all of this. A group of curious women wanting to go down beneath a building with grandiose ideas of what story or adventure they could find.

"Does our handsome Deputy Sheriff know about this?" JoJo asked.

"Yes. Thanks to his over-eager daughter who let it spill, he now does."

JoJo chuckled. "Ah, to be that young again. Little to no thoughts of caution. Just jump right into things."

Sadie had never felt that way, younger or currently, and she certainly didn't see JoJo that way. She was solid. Dependable. A person who thought through every step of life, not taking risks or chances. It was safe. And Sadie liked safe.

"What did you jump into when you were younger, JoJo?" Sadie searched her aunt's face as she asked the question. She didn't know much about JoJo before Sadie came along, and she felt bad that it was only now that she thought of asking.

JoJo shrugged. "I can't say I actually jumped, but I considered it." Her hands were folded in her lap, her thumbs rubbing together. She took a breath in and let it out with a sigh. "And I'm glad I didn't. Leaping would not have been the right decision. I'm happy with my feet firmly planted." She smiled at Sadie, but her eyes held a sadness Sadie hadn't seen before. Regret? Something she had wanted in the past but wasn't able to have?

It was clear there was more to that story than JoJo was telling, but Sadie could see her aunt's energy fading. It wasn't time to push her for details.

"I think we both need to head to bed," Sadie said. She uncurled her legs and stood. She put out a hand for JoJo, who put her recliner into a sitting position and stood, taking Sadie's hand.

"I agree. It sounds as if you've had a big day, and I am definitely tuckered out."

Sadie hugged her aunt goodnight then waited to turn off lights and lock up the house until JoJo was back in her room and settled.

Climbing the stairs each evening used to be something Sadie loved. The promise of a long, hot bath, a good book tucked under her covers, and a night of sleep in her own bed was the perfect ending to each day.

More and more, that climb was beginning to feel like a heavy slog. Stacks of bills waiting for her on her desk in the office, as well as sleepless nights worrying about how she was going to make it all work. And now she had this secret staircase in the floor of the store. What in the world could that mean?

Yes, she was curious. Yes, she entertained fun stories in her mind. But the reality couldn't be as exciting as what she imagined. And with her luck, it could bring even more things to worry about.

As she washed her face and crawled into pajamas, she thought of the look on Maddie's face, the energy from the young woman. And she laughed a bit at the look on James' face when he found out about all of it. He'd turned from relaxed to protective cop mode in mere seconds, and Sadie found she liked it. She liked it a lot.

She pulled back her covers and crawled into bed, snuggling down under the plush comforter she loved. White with yellow flowers on it, it was just the right weight and softness to burrow under and get lost in sleep.

As her eyes got heavy and she began to drift off, it wasn't bills or secret passageways that were foremost in her thoughts. It was the look in James' eyes when he asked her what kind of man he was to her. Words like gorgeous, thoughtful, and safe were the last things she remembered before drifting off to sleep.

* * *

Although the nights tended to give Sadie time to worry about the problems she had no idea how to solve, the days were busy enough to keep her distracted. Not so distracted that she didn't have moments where James' smile entered her thoughts or that her curiosity didn't get piqued when she passed the stack of books that covered the floor where the trapdoor was, but any of those thoughts were fleeting. More and more of the Homecoming crowd came in, causing business in the store to pick up. Something Sadie would never complain about. Not only was the extra business good for the balance sheet, but she also enjoyed seeing old friends as well as making new ones with the tourists who came to see the leaves change color and the vibrant hues of the season.

Before she knew it, it was time to clean up and lock up for the day. As promised, Kenny had come for a bit in the afternoon and seemed to enjoy helping customers carry items to their cars when he wasn't helping Moira dust. It didn't take long to see her first impression was right: Kenny was a good kid, just one who made a mistake – a mistake Sadie had a feeling many young boys make in their lifetime when it comes to playing catch near glass windows.

Maddie had texted earlier that day, saying she felt terrible about it but couldn't come by that afternoon. There had been an issue with the class float they were building for

Homecoming, and she needed to stay at school to help get things fixed.

That wasn't an issue for Sadie. She had a feeling Maddie would be more focused on what she'd found under the carpet than actually going through stacks of books. As much as she enjoyed Maddie's company, she felt she would have spent a lot of her day keeping the girl on task.

"Goodnight, Sadie," Ned said, pulling Sadie from her thoughts.

"Have a good evening, Ned." She returned a wave as he walked out the back door. Ned had come to her about a year ago asking if she needed any help. A retired fireman said he was bored and volunteered to help her around the shop, whether it be loading deliveries or small handyman things that needed to be done. She insisted on paying him, but he said he lived a simple, comfortable life and just wanted something to do, as well as give back to his community. His wife was a schoolteacher, and he teased that we would be doing her a favor, getting him out of the house and keeping him from turning into a bored, old grump. Moira said they just don't make 'em like Ned anymore, and Sadie agreed.

"You good if I head out?" Moira asked. She came up beside Sadie who was behind the counter near the register. "Most everything is cleaned and prepped for opening tomorrow."

"Of course. I'll get any paperwork settled, then lock

up."

The two women hugged and said goodnight to one another.

Moira went out the back door as Sadie gathered up all the receipts and papers she needed to take to the office. She stacked them on the edge of the counter so she could grab them after she locked the doors before tucking herself away to do the bookkeeping.

As she made her way to the front door to lock it, the stack of books caught her eye. She turned her attention to where the trapdoor was. Making her way over, she looked around to be sure Moira was gone and she was alone.

Her heart began to beat a little faster as she moved the stack of books and then knelt down to peel back the rug. The sight of the trapdoor almost surprised her, as if it might not still be there. As if the whole situation had been a figment of her imagination, just some strange dream she'd concocted.

She pulled the handle up from where it was tucked in and pulled. The door creaked as it opened. It looked exactly as it had when she and Maddie had peered down into it the day before. Was that really just yesterday? Sadie shook her head. She looked over toward the counter, a vague memory of a flashlight being in one of the drawers, but feared she would chicken out if she got up to look for it. It wasn't as if she was going to go down the stairs anyway.

Or was she?

Taking her phone from the back pocket of her jeans, she flipped on the flashlight and pointed it down into the hole in the floor. It illuminated the wooden staircase, but that was about it. It couldn't hurt to just see if the steps were stable, right? Maybe just flash the light down whatever passageway was down there, if any?

She put a bit of weight on the first step, and it held. She did the same with the next one and then the next as she slowly made her way down one step at a time.

Her feet met the dirt, and with her heart pounding in her chest, she held up her phone to light her way. It was a passageway of some kind, but with the short range of her phone flashlight, she couldn't see how far it went. She would just take a few steps, just to see if she could tell how long a passage it might be.

Gravel crunched under her boots as she stretched out her hand that held her phone, trying to get light to shine further.

A rumbling sound from above caused her to jump, her phone falling to the ground and landing so the light shone down. The passageway became almost black; the only light was a faint sliver coming from the store through the trapdoor.

Adrenaline raced through her system as she squatted down, her hands scrambling along the ground to find her phone.

"Ouch!" She cried out as her hand scraped against

something on the ground.

"Sadie?"

James.

"Sadie!" His voice was behind her as her hand found her phone and she turned it over. A sweep of light from the flashlight illuminated what looked like broken glass.

"Are you hurt?" He helped her stand and then pulled her into his arms.

"I'm fine." She wiped strands of hair away from her cheek that had fallen forward as she'd searched for her phone.

James had a small flashlight in his hand. He turned it face up like a torch so she could see his face. His eyes were wide, filled with concern. "No. You're not. You're bleeding."

"What? I'm…what?" She looked down at her hand.

James cupped her face with his hand, his thumb rubbing across her cheek. The other still held the flashlight. "Your face. There's blood on your face."

"Oh. It's my…hand. I wiped my hair away…"

He tucked a lock of her hair behind her ear so he could see her cheek better, his hand still gently moving across her skin.

"I'm fine, really. I…"

Before she could finish her sentence, his lips were on hers. The hand that held the flashlight came around her waist, the other still cradling her face. The warmth of his lips on hers, the intense bolt of electricity that moved through her made all else around them disappear. She was no longer in some dirty passageway beneath her store. She was floating on air, the tenderness of his touch, the warmth of his arms around her all she could notice or feel.

He pulled back and put his forehead against hers, his eyes closed. His breathing was rapid, as was hers, but from the kiss or the adrenaline she wasn't sure. Maybe both.

"You scared me to death." He turned so she was beside him, his arm holding her close to his side. "Let's get you out of here."

She nodded, words failing her for a myriad of reasons.

She went up the stairs first as James held up his flashlight to show her the way.

Sadie reached the fresh air of the store and sat down, leaning against the wall nearby. Her mind raced. After finding a legitimate passageway under her store and having James Larsen kiss her, she wasn't quite sure what emotion to address first.

James emerged from the opening and sat beside her. Both of them were still breathing hard.

"I thought you said you would wait to go in there."

She shrugged. "I was curious."

James ran a hand through his hair then rested his hands on his bent knees. "The women I care about will be the end of me."

His voice was almost a whisper, but Sadie heard it all

the same. She covered a smile with her fingers. The movement reminded her of her of the cut on her hand and she winced.

James turned at the sound. He held her hand gently in his. "Do you have a first aid kit?"

She nodded. "Behind the counter."

He retrieved it and sat beside her again to tend to her cut. Thankfully, it wasn't too deep; a bit of ointment and a bandage were all she needed.

James boxed up the kit and set it aside.

"Sadie."

The tenderness in his voice made her ache for him to kiss her again, not to mention the look in his eyes when they met hers.

"Yes."

"I need you to promise me two things." He held up a finger. "One. Don't ever scare me like that again." He held up a second finger. "And two. Do *not* tell my daughter there is actually a secret passageway. I don't get enough sleep as it is worrying about that kid. If she knows for sure she found something underneath this building..." he shook his head.

Sadie chuckled. "I promise."

He took her non-bandaged hand in his and linked their fingers together, then rested them on his outstretched leg. "And one more. Promise me you will *not* go down there again without me."

"I promise." She laid her head on his shoulder and

sighed. At that moment, Sadie didn't want to go anywhere or do anything without James nearby, a thought that warmed her heart.

Maybe the idea of letting love into her life wasn't so scary after all.

11

SADIE HARDLY SAW James after that evening. He'd helped her lock up and said goodnight, a tender brush of his lips on her injured hand before he left. They hadn't spoken about the kiss, and they hadn't had a chance to since. He dropped off Maddie on Thursday to work on the books, but that was the most they'd seen each other.

It was finally Friday night. Excitement bubbled up in Sadie as she parked her truck in the high school parking lot and made her way with the crowd toward the football field. The Friday night lights glimmered in the dusky sky, a beacon announcing that the Homecoming game would begin soon.

She said hello to Ned's wife in the ticket booth before she bought her ticket and entered the stadium. Climbing the steps to where she and Charlie had agreed to meet, she tucked her hands into her heavy coat, grateful she'd worn it, along with a scarf and beanie. She could already see her breath in the cold night air as she found Charlie, who waved her over, a saved spot on the bleachers beside her.

"You made it just in time," Charlie shouted over the noise of the pep band as well as the crowd.

"I did. I always forget how long parking can take." Sadie hugged her friend then reached to hug Davis who was on Charlie's other side.

"It's the biggest night in Nearlake, I think," Davis said with a grin as they all sat down.

"I'm not sure what that says about us," Charlie teased.

"That we have school spirit and pride," Sadie offered with a smile.

"Nearlake most certainly has that," Davis said.

Sadie smiled at her friends. Davis had blond hair cut short, blue eyes, and a bright smile. He was tall and had played basketball in high school. Charlie had been an athlete as well, playing volleyball and softball. The only reason Charlie and Sadie had become friends was that Charlie was also a big-time reader and had spent almost as much time in the library as Sadie had.

"Let's go, Huskies!" Davis shouted through hands cupped around his mouth.

The team made their way onto the field, the crowd erupting with applause as the players ran through a line made by the cheerleaders and students that went from the locker room tunnel out to almost the fifty-yard line. She wasn't sure how it was possible, but the band got even louder as they stood to play the school's fight song. The crowd sang along, each student and alumni knowing every word.

As they settled back into their seats, Sadie caught sight of James on the sidelines with the players. Dressed in jeans and a jacket with the team logo on the front, he was talking to a group of boys. Two of them had their helmets on, the others with theirs dangling from their hands by the face mask. James was smiling, saying something to them that Sadie could see got them to relax a bit. She imagined that Homecoming in Nearlake might feel like a college game to these kids, the pressure to win as palpable as the noise.

Maddie had mentioned to Sadie that her dad helped out with the team. He was not an official coach; he just offered to help during practice and give encouragement during games.

Seeing him on the field caused memories to stir in Sadie's mind. Memories tamped down over time. Memories of her sitting in those very same grandstands, cheering on the Huskies, James being a prominent reason for their victories.

But Sadie was no fool. She was far from the only girl who'd had a crush on him then. She probably wasn't the only woman in Nearlake interested in him now. But just like any other girl who dreamed of being his girlfriend, as soon as he'd hugged Tiffany when the games were over, the fantasy died.

The memories played in her mind as if on an old movie screen that was faded and worn, the details now lost to time. However, the details of James holding Sadie close in the dark beneath her store, his lips against hers, his hand cradling her face, were crystal clear.

Part of her wanted to ask him why he'd kissed her. Another part of her simply wanted to let things be. Maybe he'd only kissed her because he was caught up in the moment, adrenaline spurring the action. And yet, he'd sat and held her hand after they'd come out of the passageway until they both calmed down, the gentle kiss he placed on her injured hand just as romantic as the kiss on her lips. Maybe more so.

She looked down at her hand. It hadn't been a deep cut; a band-aid was plenty to keep it clean as it healed. The skin on her hands was getting red from the cold, so she took gloves from her pocket and put them on.

Charlie looked over as she did so. "What happened to your hand?"

Sadie mentally winced, not wanting to go into detail with Charlie just yet about the passageway or cellar. Or James.

"Just cut myself at work. No biggie."

Charlie made a sympathetic noise and turned her

attention back to the game. It wasn't unusual for Sadie to have a bump here or bruise there from her job. Moving furniture and large items was a daily occurrence.

She was just grateful her friend didn't press her for more information.

The crowd stood and cheered as the Huskies received the kickoff. The game was underway. Sadie settled into the familiar setting, her best friend beside her, the evening filled with positive energy her mind could focus on rather than the worries that weighed her down when she allowed herself too much time to think. As the game progressed, she chatted with Charlie when it wasn't too loud, but also she spent a lot of time watching James on the sidelines. He clapped for guys coming off the field, patting them on the helmet and giving them what Sadie knew were words of encouragement.

"Looks like someone's caught your attention there, Sades."

Sadie turned at the sound of the nickname. The only person who ever called her that was *"Anne!"*

She looked up to see the friend she hadn't seen in too many years.

"You know you two are the only ones I let call me that," Anne said, pointing to Sadie and Charlie.

The three women squealed and then grabbed one another in a group hug. With all the commotion around them over the game, no one noticed. Well, Davis noticed. He simply chuckled at them and then went back to watching the game.

"You're here! I cannot believe it, but you're actually here!" Charlie said as they all sat down, Anne on one side and Charlie on the other with Sadie in the middle. The row of people was accommodating and scooched down to make room.

"In the flesh." Anne held up her hands.

"Wait, what do you mean only we can call you Anne?" Sadie asked. "That's your name."

"You know her name is Annabell, but don't you remember an email a few months ago saying she's going by Annabella?" Charlie said, adding a flair to her tone when she said the name.

Sadie remembered that when they were young, most people called her Anniebell. She also remembered Anne getting to a point where she hated that. Said it sounded too country for her taste. Sadie wasn't sure what was so wrong with country, but looking at her friend, she could see the way she dressed and carried herself was much more Annabella than Anniebell. Her auburn hair flowed down her back in perfect waves. Her hat was a fur-lined snow beanie, the fur matching the cuffs of her long wool coat. Tall black leather boots fit perfectly over her legging-clad legs. The diamond on her left hand had a similar glare as the lights above and was almost as big. Other than the playful glimmer in her blue eyes, the Anne Sadie remembered was a shadow hidden behind the person who sat beside her now.

"I'm right here, Charlie. You don't have to remind me what my name is," Anne teased.

Charlie reached across Sadie and swatted Anne's arm. "What are you doing here?"

Anne waved a hand across the crowd. "What do you mean? It's Homecoming."

Sadie and Charlie both stared at her.

"Okay, okay. I don't normally come home for Homecoming," Anne conceded.

"You *never* come home for Homecoming," Sadie said, the joy over having her friend right next to her still mixing with the shock that… her friend was sitting right next to her.

Anne simply shrugged.

"No matter what the reason, we're glad you're here," Charlie said.

"Agreed." Sadie smiled.

The three women looked toward the field as the buzzer went off, signaling the end of the first half.

"Yay! It's halftime." Charlie said, clapping. "I love seeing what the kids do with the floats each year."

Sadie found James again, this time with his arm around a kid whose shoulders were slumped, his eyes looking at the ground.

"Looks like I was right," Anne said to Sadie. "Someone *has* caught your attention."

Sadie shook her head, not wanting to engage in that

conversation with Anne during the game.

As the teams began to walk to the locker rooms, the announcer said over the loudspeaker, "And let's give a round of applause to our own hometown superstar, James Larsen!"

The crowd erupted into applause as Sadie watched James. While only moments before, he'd been focused on lifting the young player's spirits, his face now looked strained. He gave a smile and a slight wave to the crowd but then made his way closer to the sideline and out of the spotlight. It wasn't hard to see that James wasn't a guy who loved the limelight, but there was something more to his struggle to embrace that moment, and Sadie wanted to know what it was.

"Excuse me. I'll be back in a minute," Sadie said as she stood and stepped past Anne.

She heard a faint, "See. Told you I was right," as she walked away.

She shook her head and smiled, knowing she'd have to face Anne's questions about James at some point, but she pushed that to the back of her mind as she went to look for him.

Making her way down the bleachers and along the field level, she scanned the crowd. Not seeing him, she realized he may have joined the team in the locker room. Taking one last look around, she spotted him walking around behind the grandstands, his hands in his pockets and his head down.

She followed, finding him all alone, leaning his back against a wall behind the bleachers.

"Hey, you." She walked up beside him and copied his stance, the two of them looking out through a tall chain link fence into the parking lot.

"Hey."

"You okay?"

"I'm fine."

She nodded but said nothing.

They stood there for a few minutes, not saying anything. If he needed to talk, he would. Sadie just wanted to be near him. Let him know he wasn't alone. The announcer's voice echoed in the night as he introduced the first float of the evening done by the freshman class.

James ran a hand through his hair and pushed away from the wall. He turned and faced Sadie. "I know I should be grateful. I've always had such strong support from this community. But…" He kicked the dirt with the toe of his boot.

Sadie waited for him to continue.

"But they don't know the truth."

"And what is the truth?"

He shook his head. "I'm not the superstar they think I am. I'm not the Golden Boy with the perfect life, the perfect career the way they imagine."

"None of us has anything perfect," Sadie offered with a shrug.

He looked down at the ground. "It's just not the whole story."

"I don't know the whole story, James. But I think it's pretty easy to know you."

His eyes met hers.

"This town celebrates your accomplishments as a football player, yes," she continued. "And it's okay to soak that in. You had a great career."

He looked away, then back at her again, his frown carrying the weight of whatever was bothering him.

"But I don't think anyone expects you to be a perfect person with a perfect life."

He took a deep breath in and let it out. "It sure feels that way sometimes."

She pushed away from the wall and stepped over to him, taking his hands in hers. "I'm sure there have been people in your life who wanted to be in your life because of your success. But there are plenty of people who want to be in your life because of the person you are. The man you are."

His lips formed a small smile at that, but it didn't last. "Like I said, there's more to the story."

"I've been told I'm a good listener."

"You are. But I gotta be honest, talking isn't what I want to do right now." He let go of her hands and cupped her face in his.

The music and noise of the night faded into the

background as he placed his lips on hers. The first time in the passageway, there'd been an urgency to his kiss, almost a need for him to be as close to her as possible to know she was okay. This time, it was a slow, searing intensity between them that warmed her all the way to her toes. Her arms wrapped around his waist, her body sinking into his as if she were made to be there.

Sadie lost all track of time or rational thought, her mind only able to focus on being held by James, as if there was no one else in the entire world she was meant to kiss but him.

When he pulled away and placed his forehead on hers, they were both breathless.

"It's official. I definitely love to do that more than talk," James said.

Sadie laughed, her breath a cloud in the cold air.

The announcer came over the loudspeaker to announce the presentation of the float for the sophomore class.

James smiled down at Sadie, her face still cradled in his hands. "As much as I hate to say it—and I mean *really* hate to say it—I need to go." He kissed her forehead. "Maddie will kill me if I don't see the float she helped work on all week."

Sadie nodded. "I understand."

James stepped back, taking her hands in his. "Thank you for coming to find me."

"You're welcome. I'm here any time you ever want to…talk."

He laughed at that and then kissed her gloved hands and then her cheek. "A very tempting offer, Sadie. I hope you mean it."

Oh, she meant it. If she wasn't falling for James Larsen before, she certainly was now.

"I mean it."

"Good." With that, he took her hand and walked her back to the stadium, the two of them parting ways as he headed to the field and she into the stands.

12

SADIE STROLLED TOWARD Lily Pad Café after church,
fallen leaves crunching under her boots as she walked.
Where the previous week had been a bustle of activity for
Homecoming, the streets of Nearlake felt like a ghost town,
complete with a piece of paper floating across the road on
the breeze. Festivities had finished the day before, people
traveling back to the places they now called home while
locals stayed home to recover before another work week
began.

Other than a couple of text messages the day before,
Sadie hadn't talked to James, but it was safe to say that he
was all she could think about. Her spirits were as light as her
steps from the thought of his kisses and the intense sea of

blue in his eyes whenever he looked at her. She still found it hard to believe that James Larsen could have any level of interest in her, but after Friday night, any doubts she had were fading fast.

It hadn't been lost on her either that the moment they shared was behind the bleachers of their alma mater. The very place she'd spent dreaming that one day, someone as amazing as James Larsen would even glance her way. And now, as she headed to meet her closest friends for lunch, she – Sadie Woods – could say she'd been kissed by him during a football game behind the grandstands.

She laughed out loud. From joy? From the irony of it all? It didn't matter. For the first time in too long, she was happy.

As she opened the door to Lily's and stepped inside, her heart warmed in her chest even more at the sight of Charlie and Anne sitting at "their" table. Sadie still couldn't wrap her head around the fact that her friend was there in person. Having a flair for the dramatic, it wasn't unlike Anne to just show up the way she did, but Sadie still couldn't dismiss the tiny red flag raised in her mind as she wondered why her friend had really come home.

However, for now, she was grateful Anne was back, and Sadie planned to soak up every moment she could while she had the chance.

"Hey, you two," she said as she approached the table and hung her coat and purse on the back of her chair.

"Hey!" They both said in unison.

Sadie leaned down to hug them both before taking a seat.

"Charlie was just catching me up on the kids. I can't believe one is out of college and the other halfway through," Anne said.

Anne had the most beautiful, naturally curly hair. Sadie noticed she now straightened it, giving her a more polished look. In some ways, it is more severe. Her makeup was flawless; her outfit looked brand new. Her perfectly manicured nails wrapped around a coffee mug in front of her. It all matched her current demeanor, but not the young woman Sadie had known who had been happiest with little to no makeup, spending most of her days riding horses, her gorgeous auburn hair flowing behind her in the wind.

Granted, Sadie and Charlie weren't exactly who they'd been twenty-plus years ago, but the perfectly put-together woman she saw now didn't feel like a natural progression. It felt…forced.

Sadie knew Anne's husband, Leo, was extremely wealthy. They moved in high-end circles, and Sadie could guess the influence that they had on Anne. It was more of an observation than judgment. While many of Anne's emails or social media updates portrayed the "perfect" life, the person who sat with them now looked a bit tired, her eyes not as bright as Sadie remembered.

"Tell me about it. I'm their mother. I fight the feeling

that I'm ancient every day," Charlie said, then took a sip of her coffee.

"You don't look a day over thirty," Anne encouraged.

Charlie laughed. "I have missed you for a lot of reasons, but how you lie to me is in the top five."

Anne laughed and then turned her attention to Sadie. "And now that you're here, I would love for you to update me on what's going on between you and our hunky hometown hero."

Charlie leaned forward in her chair. "Oooh, I want that update, too."

"You mean you don't already know?" Anne asked Charlie.

Charlie shook her head. "We haven't had much of a chance to talk lately."

"Wait. I thought you two talked every day," Anne said to Charlie.

Charlie shrugged. "We've been busy. And quite frankly, I can't seem to get this one to open up about our fine Deputy Sheriff." She jerked her thumb at Sadie, the two women talking as if Sadie wasn't even there. "But I *do* know that she had dinner at his house the other night and that his daughter is working at the store."

Sadie's cheeks flushed as the two of them turned their attention toward her. "How do you know all of that?"

"You're avoiding the question, but I will humor you," Charlie said. "As I told you, I volunteer at the high school library, and Maddie is quite the reader. She chatted with me the other day about the book you gave her and how much she's enjoying working in the store. She also mentioned you delivered a dresser the other night and stayed for dinner."

"Oh, my. Date night at the Sheriff's house," Anne said as she shifted in her chair to face Sadie more. "I definitely want to hear more details."

Sadie fought the urge to roll her eyes as she took a sip of her water. She set down her glass and faced her friends. "Okay, you two," she said with a laugh. It was hard not to, with them both eyeing her like teenagers at the lunch table, eager for the gossip of the day. "First of all, it was hardly a date. I gave Maddie a ride home after work, and as a thank you for doing so, as well as delivering the dresser for her, *she* invited me to dinner."

"Was the gorgeous guy you've been in love with since high school at this dinner?" Anne asked, her eyes now twinkling with a bit of mischief.

Although she wasn't thrilled with the line of questioning, Sadie liked seeing her friend perk up a bit, shades of her former self emerging as she talked.

"Okay, love is a strong word. I'll admit I had a crush on the guy when I was a kid, but half the girls in town did."

Anne shrugged. "That's true. But none of them are having dinner at his house now, are they?" She wiggled her eyebrows and then took another sip of coffee.

Sadie shook her head and laughed. "Not that I'm aware

of, no."

"I would also like to know where you disappeared to during halftime of the game Friday night," Charlie said.

While her friends had sounded like teenagers in their inquisition, Sadie now felt like one as her face flushed with heat, her mind recalling the kiss she and James had shared.

"Okay. I'm not sure I've ever seen you blush like that," Anne said.

"Me neither," Charlie agreed.

"Okay! Okay! I was with James behind the bleachers, and he kissed me." Not one to share much of anything in her life, Sadie couldn't keep the words from rushing out of her mouth before she covered her face with her hands.

"No way!" Charlie exclaimed.

"Way to go, Sades," Anne said.

Sadie moved her hands away from her face, her mouth now in a wide smile as she laughed. "I can't believe I'm telling you all of this." She shook her head and took another sip of water. "I feel like I'm sixteen."

Charlie sat back in her chair and smiled. "But that's gotta feel pretty awesome, though, right?"

"His kiss or feeling sixteen?" Anne said with a grin.

"Both," Sadie said.

"I cannot believe I didn't know any of this," Charlie said.

"It only happened Friday night, and I didn't see you yesterday. It didn't feel like the kind of thing I should text you about."

Charlie nodded. "You're forgiven."

"And the first time was really more just…" Sadie said, then pursed her lips together.

"The first time?" her friends said in unison.

Well, that cat was out of the bag.

Sadie's shoulders sagged. She couldn't decide if she wanted to laugh or cry. Maybe both. It honestly felt good to have her friends to talk to. Until that moment, she hadn't realized how much she'd been keeping to herself. With all that had been happening with James and Maddie, she hadn't thought much about her financial woes. And she never meant to keep so much from Charlie, especially. But she sure could use her friends right now.

"Okay. It wasn't the first time he kissed me."

Anne and Charlie leaned forward again, their elbows on the table as Sadie talked. "It's all been happening so fast. There was the supposed break-in at the store, then Maddie helping me with the shop and finding an underground passageway, and then I went down there, and that's where James kissed me for the first time, although I think that was mainly because he was relieved I was okay but…" she waved her hand as if to bat that thought away. "And then Friday night, I was just trying to listen as he worked through something he was struggling with, and the next thing I know, we were kissing and…" she stopped and sighed.

Anne's mouth dropped open. "Wow. That was… a lot.

How long have I been gone?"

"Too long," Sadie and Charlie said in unison.

"But this all happened like last week," Charlie said.

Sadie nodded.

"I'm sorry. All of that you just spewed only happened this past week?" Anne raised her eyebrows and pointed at Sadie.

Sadie and Charlie both nodded.

It was clear she would have to elaborate, but for the moment, Sadie felt a weight lifted.

"Okay, okay," Anne said. "Let's take one thing at a time. A supposed break-in at the store?" She held up a finger to tick off the first subject.

"Yes," Sadie said. "But it was just a kid who hit a baseball through the back door window. It's all fine. That's all good."

"Okay, then, two." Anne held up another finger. "Did I hear you right? You said secret passageway?"

Sadie nodded. "Yes. Maddie found a trapdoor in the floor. It leads down to a passageway under the shop."

"Wow." Charlie blinked as she took it all in.

"We will come back to that one," Anne said. "And three, James kissed you then as well as Friday night."

"Yes."

"Sheesh, woman. You've lived most of a novel in only a week's time," Anne said.

Sadie laughed at that.

Lily came over to their table. "It's good to see the three of you in here again together. And laughing."

The three of them smiled at her.

"Your usual order?"

"Yes, please," Sadie and Charlie answered.

"I'd love just a cup of your soup, please, Lily," Anne said.

"You got it."

Once she was gone, the three women sat back in their chairs. For a few moments, no one said anything.

Had Sadie shared too much? It felt good to be able to process some of it with her friends, but maybe she should have kept the part about the passageway to herself.

"Initially, I was glad to have lunch with you both today, but I fear that a couple of hours at this table isn't going to be nearly enough to unpack all that was just laid out on the table," Charlie said, breaking the silence.

They all laughed.

"I'm sorry. I didn't mean to verbally vomit it like that," Sadie admitted. "There's just been a...lot happening." She had a fleeting thought of the stacks of bills in her desk drawer she was trying to solve but pushed it aside. She'd shared enough for one day.

"I'm happy for you," Anne said with a smile. "James is a good guy. I can't say I know him all that well now, but he always seemed genuine. You deserve someone who is good to you, Sades."

"Thanks, Anne," Sadie said with a smile. "I'm not sure what it all means just yet, but I'm not as scared as I was to find out."

As Anne took a sip of her coffee, Sadie couldn't help but notice the sparkle in Anne's eyes fading once more.

Charlie sat back in her chair with her legs crossed and her arms crossed as well.

"I know that look," Sadie said. "What are you churning in that brain of yours?"

Charlie quirked her mouth to one side, then spoke. "As much as I want to know more about you and James Larsen, my mind is stuck on this passageway you mentioned beneath the store."

"I asked JoJo about it, but she didn't know anything. She said my grandparents never mentioned it."

"You said you went down into it. That was when James kissed you the first time," Charlie said.

"Yes." Sadie fought to hold back a grin. Would she ever be able to talk about James or think about him without everything inside her lighting up or heating up? She hoped not. But it would be nice if her traitorous facial expressions wouldn't give away every emotion she was feeling.

"And what did you find?"

"Nothing, really. I just took a few steps to see how far it went, and then I dropped my phone, and James came down and wanted us to get out of there. He said it was too dangerous."

"I have to say, I agree with James," Anne said. "I'm as curious as you are, but just going down there, especially alone, wasn't your finest hour, Sades."

"I was fine. And I wasn't going to go any further. I just wanted to see if it was an actual passageway or... I don't know," she said with a shrug.

Charlie tapped a finger against her chin. "I bet the library has some archives or historical things we could find to see if there is anything documented about it."

"I was going to do that; I just haven't had the time," Sadie said.

"I do. I'd be happy to check things out for you," Charlie offered.

"Would you? That would be great."

"Of course." Charlie leaned forward and placed a hand on Sadie's arm.

"I'd do anything for you, you know that."

Sadie smiled, humbled by her friend's statement.

"I'll help, too!" Anne said, sitting up in her chair and patting Sadie's other arm.

"You will?" Sadie and Charlie said together.

"Don't sound so surprised! I love Sadie, too, and I'm happy to help."

"I just thought you wouldn't be here that long," Charlie said.

"Well," Anne's shoulders sagged a little. "I'm not sure how long I'll be here, but while I am here, I want to help

Sadie."

Sadie couldn't fight the feeling her friend wasn't telling them everything, but what she did know about Anne was that if they pressed her for info, she'd only shut down and say less.

"I appreciate it, Anne." Sadie took her friend's hand and squeezed it. "I'm glad you're home."

13

AS JAMES DROVE his truck to Sadie's house, he felt like a teenager about to pick up a girl for their first date. It had been a long time since he'd been interested in anyone, and the warmth in his chest at the mere thought of Sadie was welcomed over the emptiness he'd felt for far too long. Of course, his daughter was in the seat beside him, so the evening would be far from a date, but James would take every second possible near Sadie.

She'd texted him the day before asking if he wouldn't mind helping her fix a few things around the house, and he'd jumped at the chance to say yes. It helped that Tuesday was his day off. She couldn't leave the store until late afternoon, so she'd invited him and Maddie over for dinner.

She'd said the company would be good for her aunt as well. Eager to spend time with Sadie, James also looked forward to meeting JoJo. He'd heard a lot about how kind and giving she was and had a feeling Sadie was an apple that hadn't fallen far from that family tree.

He glanced over at Maddie and then back to the road. He could see what a positive influence Sadie had had on Maddie's life, even in the short time she'd been helping at the store. An evening with JoJo would be good for her as well. His heart sank a little at the thought of Maddie not having her mom around. His sister-in-law was great, and Maddie loved spending time with his mom, but beyond that, Maddie didn't have a lot of women in her life. He was grateful to Sadie for spending time with her.

He was glad to have her in his life as well. And no one was more surprised than he was at how easily his heart opened at the chance with Sadie. Even though the calendar might say things were moving fast with them, to him, it was all a natural progression of his feelings for her, and he could only hope she felt the same.

He had to admit that when he'd kissed her the first time in the passageway, quite a bit of it was fueled by adrenaline. Finding her down there alone and then seeing she'd been hurt almost gutted him. He'd wanted nothing more than to hold her as close as possible, to know at his very core that she was truly okay. When she'd looked up at him, her face cradled in his hand, there was nothing to hold him back from placing his lips on hers.

Best decision he'd made in a long time.

He rubbed his chin with one hand as the other guided the steering wheel of his truck. When the announcer at the football game had drawn attention to James at halftime, it had taken all his strength to force a smile and wave to the crowd. Feeling as if he might throw up, he'd gone behind the grandstands to give himself a minute to regain some composure.

When he'd turned to see Sadie there, his roiling emotions had calmed. Taking pride in the fact that he was good at hiding his feelings, it hadn't eluded him that she'd noticed something was wrong and came to find him. He hadn't intended to say anything to her, but she had a tendency to get him to talk more than he was used to. He'd meant it, though, that kissing her was much more enjoyable than talking. The memory of holding her again, her lips sweet and warm against his…

"Why are you grinning like that?" Maddie asked, snapping him from his thoughts.

James blinked, bringing his mind back to the present. He shook his head. Looking like a love-struck fool in front of his daughter before knowing exactly what was going on between him and Sadie was not his best move.

"No reason."

He pulled the truck into Sadie's driveway, grateful for the easy change of subject, as well as the short attention span of a teenager. Especially one who was into houses.

"Wow. This place is so pretty." Maddie said, her eyes wide as she took in the sight of Sadie's house. "It's like the perfect farmhouse off the show *Home Town* or something."

James had to agree. Everything about it screamed Sadie, from the warm glow of the lights in the window to the pumpkins and happy scarecrow on the front porch; the whole thing said, "Welcome. Come inside and visit."

He didn't mind if he did.

Maddie hopped out of the truck as James did the same. He grabbed his toolbox from the truck bed and followed Maddie up the front steps. Before they reached the front door, it opened.

"Hey, you two. Welcome."

James' mouth pulled into a grin like an idiot, but he didn't care. Seeing her was like having the sun break through the clouds, all warmth and light that shot straight to his heart. She was in jeans and a white buttoned-down shirt, her hair pulled up into one of those messy buns, as Maddie called it, and her feet were bare, her toes painted a bright yellow. Well, didn't that just complete the whole soft, sexy package that stood in front of him?

"Hey, Sadie," Maddie said, then gave her a hug.

James blinked. Completely smitten or not, it was time to pull it together. Standing on her front porch, drooling was not his best look.

"Thank you so much for having us over," he said as he

stepped into the house after his daughter.

"I'm the one who's grateful for your help. Making you dinner is the least I can do in return."

Maddie made her way past them. As James took another step into the front hall, Sadie closed the door and turned. They were face to face, close enough that if he leaned down just a little, he could steal a kiss. Her face was turned up, her eyes looking at his mouth as if she had the same idea.

"I'm so glad you're here!" A woman's voice echoed from the other room.

Sadie blinked, the moment gone. "Please. Come in and meet my aunt."

James nodded and followed her as she led the way, his heart pounding in his chest from her mere nearness. Maybe love-struck didn't even begin to define how he felt about this woman.

The inside of the house matched the outside, warm and welcoming. The living room had a large sofa with big cushions that asked to be sat on and sunk into. There were tones of yellow and blue all around, with spots of green and bright colors here and there via a throw pillow or blanket. Beside it was a large lounge chair; a tiny woman settled into it with a blanket over her legs.

"You must be JoJo," James said. He set his toolbox off to the side of the sofa and reached out a hand to shake. "It's nice to meet you."

"You, as well," JoJo said as she shook his hand.

"I'm Maddie." Maddie moved around him to do the same.

"Such wonderful manners. It's nice to meet you, too, Maddie," JoJo said. "We can't thank you enough for coming to help."

"I'll be honest; I was a little surprised when Sadie asked," James said, sneaking a look at Sadie, who was beside him.

Her cheeks flushed with color, but she didn't respond.

"Well, I have to admit, I'm not very good at asking for help, and I fear I've passed that trait on to my niece. But I think it's as good a reason as any to have you over for dinner," JoJo said with a wink.

"Jo…" Sadie said in a tone that matched her cheek color.

"Nothing bad about asking for help." James looked back and forth at both women. "And I'm certainly not one to turn down a free dinner."

"Did you make that quilt, Miss Woods?" Maddie asked JoJo as she took a seat at the end of the sofa next to JoJo's chair.

"Oh please, call me JoJo. Miss Woods is polite, yet a bit too stuffy for me." JoJo smiled at Maddie. "And I didn't make this one, no. A friend from my quilting group made it for me when we got my diagnosis. She wanted me to have it during radiation and recovery to wrap myself up in the warmth and comfort of those who love me."

"Wow. It is really beautiful. And that's so cool your friend did that for you."

"It is cool, isn't it?"

"I would love to know how to make something like this." Maddie ran a hand over a corner of the quilt.

"Really? If you want, I can show you how," JoJo offered.

"No way! That's awesome."

James watched as his daughter and JoJo fell into their own world discussing quilt making, and his heart warmed in his chest. He was right. JoJo was just as kind and gracious as Sadie and yet another positive influence on Maddie.

Sadie nudged his arm. "Come on," she said as she waved a hand. "Those two will talk quilting for hours, which means we can get going on the stuff I need your help with."

He grabbed his toolbox and followed her through a doorway into the kitchen.

"I really am surprised you asked me for my help," he said.

She turned and leaned a hip against the kitchen counter near the sink. As she crossed her arms in front of her, she said, "Oh yeah? Why is that?"

"Well, when I first offered my help, it wasn't hard to see you were uncomfortable with the idea."

She smiled and looked down at the floor.

"You did exactly that," he said as he moved a finger up

and down to emphasize her reaction.

She laughed. "Okay. Fair enough." She tucked a stray wisp of hair behind her ear and looked at him again. "I do have trouble asking for help."

"Why is that?" As much as James wanted to lend her a hand around the house, he ached to know more about her, to understand her as completely as possible.

She shrugged. "I grew up having to be pretty independent."

James glanced into the other room, JoJo and Maddie now looking through a stack of quilts on the sofa. He looked back at Sadie. "Has it always been just you and your Aunt?"

She nodded. "Since I was nine. She's only twelve years older than me, so it was a lot for her to take on at a young age, but she's basically all I've had in life, all I've got now."

She blinked and looked out the window that sat over the kitchen sink. He could tell she was fighting back tears. Although he wanted to know everything about her, the last thing he wanted was to upset her. If it had been her and her aunt against the world, he could only imagine what she must be feeling with JoJo's illness.

"Well, I'm just glad you asked me to help. What do we need to address first?"

She took in a deep breath and let it out, the smile she gave him, relaying gratitude for the change of subject. "First thing is the garbage disposal." She pushed away from the counter and opened the cupboards beneath the sink. "I've watched YouTube videos on how to fix it, but this time, I can't seem to quite get it going again."

James lifted an eyebrow. "I'm impressed."

"Impressed I know how to find things on YouTube or impressed I actually have some level of garbage disposal maintenance?"

Her teasing made him laugh, something he was recognizing he hadn't done in a long time, and it felt good. Everything about being with Sadie felt good. "Both."

After he took a look at the garbage disposal and fixed that, they moved into the downstairs bathroom to look at a faucet Sadie said was giving them trouble. JoJo and Maddie had since moved into a sewing room at the back of the house, the whir of a sewing machine mixed with talking and laughter floated down the hall.

Sadie sat on the edge of the bathtub as James poked around to see what the problem could be.

"I really am grateful to you for all of this. I know I'm masking it on the outside, but my insides are churning over feeling so…useless."

He stopped what he was doing and turned to her. He took a rag from his back pocket, wiped his hands, and then plopped it down on the counter before he leaned against the sink so he could face her. "First of all, you're not as good at masking your feelings as you think."

Her mouth dropped open, but then she narrowed her

eyes as she smiled.

"Second, it doesn't make you useless because you need help. You're human, Sadie. We all need help at some point in life."

"What are the things you need help with?" she asked.

He chuckled, not expecting her to turn the tables on him. "Well, I feel totally inept most days as a single father to a teenage daughter."

Sadie smiled. "You are an amazing father, James. Anyone who spends one minute with Maddie can see that."

He shook his head and looked at the bathroom door, not wanting Maddie to hear anything. It sounded like music was playing now.

"Trust me, between the music and sewing machine sounds and them talking, they can't hear us," Sadie said, reading his thoughts.

Maddie was an amazing kid. But James didn't feel he could take credit for that. He was gone so much when she was young, and then he'd failed at his marriage. What kept him from doing the same as a father?

"You wanna tell me what's going on in your mind? Based on your furrowed brow, it's quite a lot."

James crossed his arms over his chest. "I don't know. I just…"

"Doubt yourself. Feel that if you don't do everything perfectly, you will somehow mess her up?"

He met Sadie's eyes. "You a mind reader now?"

She laughed and shook her head. "Nope. I've just walked the motherhood road with Charlie since her kids were born. She says she asks herself those questions all the time."

Mark and Amber said the same things to James, yet he struggled to believe they battled the way he did. They worked hard at the marriage, and their relationship was solid. Solid was never a word James would have used to describe his relationship with Tiffany.

"You said the other night at the football game that no one knew the truth. What did you mean by that?"

James eyed the door once more, then looked at the ground. Except for his brother, no one knew the whole story about things with Tiffany.

"I understand if you don't want to share more."

His eyes met Sadie's. The sincerity of her words, as well as her genuine heart, gave him the courage to speak.

"Things between me and Tiffany weren't as great as everyone imagines." He rubbed his chin, then tucked his hand back, his arms crossed his chest. "She loved our life in the NFL. And I did, too. Most of it. She hated when I retired and hated it even more when I became a cop. Moving to Nearlake was just the cherry on the sundae that was the downward spiral of our marriage."

Sadie nodded. "Small-town living isn't for everyone."

"It wasn't for her, that's for sure. But I just wanted...quiet. I wanted the kindness of neighbors and the respect people give us here that would allow Maddie a somewhat normal existence."

"I'm not saying you need to put up a billboard about your relationship or anything, James, but no one's relationship is perfect. It seems like you're carrying a pretty heavy weight over the reality, not fitting what others *might* believe."

He shook his head. He ran a hand through his hair and then down his face. It was close to impossible to look at Sadie as he spoke, so he chickened out and looked at the ground. "It's not just that, Sadie. I found out shortly before Tiffany's death that she was…having an affair. The night she died, she was driving back from what was a supposed girls' weekend away, but the cops told me she drove off the road because she was texting. Turns out she was seeing a former teammate of mine. She was messaging him when she drove into a tree."

The quiet in the small bathroom was deafening. James could hear his heart beating in his ears. "I failed her. I failed us. I was so intent on what I thought was best. So intent on what I wanted."

He shook his head, the memories flowing back as he spoke, his gut churning with regret. "I've never told anyone but my brother. And I intend for Maddie to never know. She doesn't need that."

He put his hands against the counter behind him, bracing himself for her response. Would she judge him or maybe throw platitudes his way? Tell him it wasn't his fault. All the stuff he tried to tell himself but could never believe.

Sadie stood and stepped in front of him. She looked him in the eye, cupped his face with one hand, and then placed a tender kiss on his cheek before wrapping her arms around him and holding him tight.

14

SADIE HELD JAMES close as if she could physically take some of the burden from him that he was carrying.

He wasn't wrong. She hated to admit it, but she had had that same image of James and his wife whenever she saw them or heard about them. Even though she knew every relationship wasn't perfect, it was hard to see couples like James and Tiffany or Charlie and Davis and not think things were all good. In the time she'd spent with James, she could see he carried the weight of grief, the pain of his wife's death unimaginable. And then add to it the heartache of losing her to another man even before she was gone.

She could try to grasp what he was feeling, but all Sadie wanted at that moment was to comfort him. It was clear in how he told his story that he not only feared judgment but judged himself to a point he didn't deserve.

His arms came around her, his cheek resting on top of her head.

Sadie's body melted into his, her heartbeat combining with his as they stood there embracing in the bathroom of her house, the sound of Maddie and JoJo chatting coming from down the hall.

She pulled back and looked up at him, still not wanting to speak. The last thing he needed right now was any kind of attempt from her to solve what hurt. There wasn't an easy solution. Sadie understood that better than anyone. No words could change that her aunt was sick, that she might lose her shop, that she'd spent her life feeling as if it was dangerous to trust her heart to anyone because people leave. Whether they died or walked away, they'd go.

Looking into James' eyes, her heart still straddled the fence of wanting to believe she could be all in with him, yet afraid to take the chance that he, too, would one day leave her. Was he willing to be all in with her? Love was messy. Look at all he'd been through already. And yes, they'd shared some amazing moments together, as well as the current one with her wrapped in his arms, but was that enough? Was it enough for him, or did he fear risking his heart as well?

He cupped her face in his hands. "I feel like there are about a million thoughts running through that head of yours right now."

She smiled and leaned her forehead against his chest. His hand held her head against him as he placed a soft kiss on the top of her head. She took a deep breath in, soaking in what it felt like to be held by a man she knew would protect her, hold her close when she needed it. Was she brave enough to believe it could be this way for more than just that moment?

"Thank you." He whispered, his breath warm against her ear.

She pulled back and looked at him again. "For what?"

"For this. For listening. For being here."

"You're welcome."

"Hey, Dad! Come and see what JoJo taught me how to make!" Maddie's voice from down the hall drew them from the moment.

Sadie stepped back from James' embrace and smiled at him. "She really is amazing, James. And so are you." She stood on her tiptoes to place a soft kiss on his lips, then headed to the kitchen to finish dinner.

* * *

It had been almost a week since that moment in the bathroom, but Sadie struggled to think of much else. It felt as if the past month had been sprinkled with moments together amid daily life that was becoming a blur of work in the shop, caring for JoJo, and all the other various things Sadie was involved in around town. Each time they were together, there was a more meaningful connection than the last, although what James had told her about his marriage to Tiffany weighed heavily on her mind.

James admitted that only Sadie and his brother knew the truth, and she was getting a clearer picture of the man behind the hometown legend. He hid his feelings well; she'd give him that. But as she got closer to James, it wasn't hard to see the soft-hearted, genuine guy behind the tough exterior he showed. Solid. Dependable. A man you could trust. Those were all true about James. But what came with those truths was a weight of living up to expectations that no one should have to try and live up to.

The rest of the evening had been filled with good food and good conversation, and it was easy to see that Maddie was just as good for JoJo as JoJo was for Maddie. It warmed Sadie to see her aunt with a huge smile on her face most of the night; Maddie's youthful energy was the best medicine possible.

Sadie could see James had relaxed as if a burden had been lifted for him by trusting her, and he and his daughter could be themselves around Sadie and JoJo.

A smile formed on Sadie's face at the thought of James and Maddie feeling safe with her. She felt safe with them as well, her heart opening more and more to the thought of both of them being a part of her life.

She parked her truck and grabbed the bag of books she wanted to donate then headed from the main parking lot of the high school across campus to the library. Charlie had called and asked her to come share a sack lunch with her, and since it was Monday and the store was closed, Sadie was happy to say yes.

With the bag of books and her purse slung over her shoulder, she tucked her hands inside her coat pocket as she walked. The breeze had a bite of cold in it, a sure sign winter was on its way. Locals had a theory that Halloween night was when the temperatures turned from cold to really cold, which was evident by how many kids were fussy over having to wear heavy coats over their costumes. Although Halloween was still a few days away, the drop in temperature was a sure sign that the theory would hold true this year.

A bell rang, and doors swung open, teenagers emerging like ants with backpacks on as they made their way from class to lunch hour. Sadie reached the library building and held the door open for two girls headed inside. The heat as she stepped inside wrapped around her like a blanket, the quiet of the library an old friend whispering to her to come in and get lost in a story.

She smiled as the two girls stopped to look at a book together on a shelf just inside the door, their heads together as they whispered to one another. Sadie mentally reminisced over the truth that those years were filled with as much wonder and curiosity as they were angst and emotion.

She made her way to the main desk, where Charlie stood staring at a computer.

"Hey, you."

"Hey!" Charlie loudly whispered back. "I'm so glad you could join me. Come on back." She waved for Sadie to follow her down a short hallway behind the main desk.

Sadie knew the library well. As a teenager, she always made sure her study hall hour was one that was held in the library, and she'd volunteered after school to help Debra, the librarian who'd worked there for more years than Sadie could fathom.

"Hi, Debra." She poked her head into the head librarian's office.

"Well, hello, Sadie." Debra sat behind a gray metal desk and looked up as she spoke. Sadie was pretty sure that desk had been there since the library was built. Debra had to be in her seventies now and still had the same bob haircut and dark-rimmed glasses, although her hair was all silver now rather than blond. "Are you here to see Charlie?" Debra asked.

"I am. We're going to have lunch."

"You enjoy. It's good to see you."

"You, too."

Sadie joined Charlie in a small kitchenette two doors down from Debra's office. It was said around town that the high school library was bigger and better than the town library, and Sadie didn't dispute that. As generous as the people of Nearlake were, their hearts and money tended to go to their alma mater before anything else, the school receiving a large cash donation when the library had been renovated and expanded a few years back.

Charlie had a small picnic set up for them at the table in the center of the room. Complete with picnic basket.

"You really know how to make a girl feel special," Sadie teased as she set her purse and bag of books on a nearby chair before taking off her coat and draping it across them. She took a seat at the table with Charlie. There were real plates and napkins, as well as a small charcuterie board complete with multiple cheeses, meats, and crackers. A small serving dish held three different kinds of olives. "Wow. You really went all out."

Panic rose in Sadie for a moment, recalling all birthdays and anniversaries that would matter to Charlie. "Is there a special occasion I'm forgetting?"

Charlie smiled as she set a cold bottle of water in front of each of them. "No. I think I just miss making meals for people."

Sadie tried to read between the lines of that comment. Although Charlie put on a brave face, Sadie knew that the empty nest years had been tougher than Charlie anticipated.

"Well, it looks amazing, and I'm grateful I'm on the receiving end of it."

Charlie's face lit up. Mission accomplished.

"So, I know you texted me about how Tuesday night's dinner, but I'm still going to do my mandatory ask you face-to-face for details," Charlie said as she made up a plate for herself.

The moment in the bathroom with James came to Sadie's thoughts, but that was the last thing she would share with anyone. James had trusted her with that information, and she intended to stick that in the vault of her mind and throw away the key. Besides, there were plenty of other parts of the evening she could share.

"It honestly was really nice. James helped me fix a few things around the house while JoJo taught Maddie how to quilt, and then we had dinner."

Charlie narrowed her eyes for a second, then shrugged. "Okay. I'll believe you. With JoJo and Maddie there, I didn't imagine there'd be any more hot kisses or make-out sessions going on between you two."

Sadie laughed out loud. "You're killing me. I should have never told you anything about James."

"Nonsense. You tell me everything. Well, almost everything."

Charlie had a rule that there were things in a relationship that belonged between those two people alone and Sadie wholeheartedly agreed. But as her best friend, Charlie did know more about her than anyone else besides JoJo.

Charlie sighed, a sadness floating across her features.

She blinked and sat up in her chair, whatever was on her mind a fleeting thought. Sadie made a note of it, though, tucking it away to ask her about another time.

"I'm glad Maddie and JoJo hit it off. Although I'm not surprised."

"Me, too." Sadie made a plate for herself as well. The spread was so beautiful she almost didn't want to mess it up.

Almost.

"You said when you invited me to lunch, you had something to tell me," Sadie said.

"Oh yes!" Charlie said around a bit of cracker and cheese, her hand in front of her mouth. She finished chewing and then wiped her hands on her napkin. "I did some digging to see if I could find anything here about the…" she leaned forward to whisper behind her hand, "…secret passageway."

Sadie chuckled. "It's okay, Char. I don't think anyone else, but Debra is back here, and she's down the hall."

"Davis has some old books that belonged to his family. I read through those."

Davis was a member of one of the founding families of Nearlake. Sadie had heard him more than once call it both a blessing and a curse.

"In those books, I read about a supposed treasure – mostly gold bars—that was buried years ago by a group of robbers whose leader was a crooked politician. Shocker, I know. But who knows? Maybe that could be why there's a tunnel under the store. Maybe there's gold down there. A true buried treasure."

"As much as I would love to think that there is gold under my store, I find that highly unlikely. And aren't there more than a few historical stories about gold in this area? We do live in Idaho."

Charlie shrugged and popped an olive in her mouth.

The mere thought of a small fortune being somewhere in the secret passageway they'd found did give Sadie pause. A fantasy of having enough to pay off all the bills that were pounding at her door faded as fast as it came. Even if she did find something of value under there, would it even belong to her? The land belonged to her current landlord, a large corporation based in Boise called Evergreen Properties.

She shook her head. Even entertaining, that thought was silly. She lived in the real world with real problems, not an adventure novel.

"All I'm saying is that it might not hurt to just see what's down there," Charlie said, pulling Sadie from her thoughts.

"I don't know. James said it could be dangerous."

Charlie scrunched up her face. "That's fair."

Sadie understood the desire for the passageway to be something exciting, and she hated being the one to pop her friend's balloon of intrigue.

"Thank you so much for looking into it, though," Sadie

said. "It means a lot to me to have your help."

"Always."

Sadie sat back in her chair and looked out the window. Why was she so hesitant to lean into her friend? Yes, Sadie was independent and used to it being her and JoJo against the world. But in all truth, she and JoJo hadn't faced anything quite like this before. After seeing what came from an evening of having James help her at the house, as well as him trust her with what weighed him down, maybe what Sadie needed most right now was to tell Charlie the truth.

"Hey. What's up?" Charlie asked. "You just went a million miles away."

Sadie looked at her friend.

Charlie leaned forward in her chair.

"I may lose the store." She hadn't meant for it to come out so blunt, but it did. It summed it all up, really.

"What?" Charlie's eyes got wide.

Sadie took a deep breath in and let it out. She looked down at her hands folded in her lap as she talked. "I received notice from my landlord that they're raising the rent, and with JoJo's medical bills, I can't swing it. I'm afraid we'll have to sell the house or try to move the store, but…" her voice trailed off. Just the thought of those things happening made her want to throw up.

"Sadie. I had no idea."

"How could you? I haven't told anyone. JoJo doesn't even know."

Charlie's eyebrows raised at that. "I knew you were a private person, but that surprises me."

Sadie shook her head. "She doesn't need added stress right now."

"But you do?"

Sadie looked at her friend. Leave it to Charlie to shoot straight. "It's not like I intentionally set out to do things alone."

"Of course you do."

Sadie's shoulders sagged as she leaned her elbows on the table, her head in her hands. "I do, don't I?"

"I'll assume that's a rhetorical question."

Sadie had to chuckle at that.

"Hey." Charlie placed a hand on Sadie's arm. "You're not alone. You know that. Deep down, you know that."

Sadie nodded. She folded her hands in front of her on the table and looked at her friend. "I just don't know what to do. If I pray any harder, I fear God's gonna get tired of hearing from me." She forced a small smile as she let a tear fall, her hand swiping it away as it made its way down her cheek.

Blessedly, Charlie said nothing, just rubbed Sadie's arm. Much like the other night with James, there was nothing Charlie could say or do to fix things. It was time for Sadie to accept fate and face what was to come, no matter how difficult.

15

SADIE SAT IN the office of Get and Gather, papers strewn across the desk, her laptop opened to various spreadsheets she was pouring over.

It had felt good to tell Charlie what was going on, but the peace from that had faded the minute she'd opened the store and then came into the office to tackle what now sat before her.

She and Charlie had talked more about the details of her situation. Talking through her options did help some. The thought of selling the house or having to move the store sounded a little less scary, and yet Sadie's stomach still turned at the thought of either choice.

History was important to her. She'd practically made it her whole life. And there was rich history for her and JoJo in their house. Her grandparents bought it years ago and raised their daughters in it, and then she and JoJo made it their home. It was all Sadie knew. They'd already had to get a mortgage on it after her grandparents passed during a time when things were tight, but business had picked up, and for years, they'd been able to make the payments until now.

And she had the same history with the store. She grew up wandering around all the furniture and lamps and knick-knacks and books. When she was little, her grandmother would let her choose whatever she wanted from the shelf of children's books they had, and then she'd curl up in a big chair and read. Watching her grandparents and JoJo visit with customers while helping them find what they were looking for were some of Sadie's favorite memories. The house and the store were more than buildings to her; they were her life. And it tore her insides apart to think she might have to sacrifice one of them to save the other.

Yes, she could always find a different spot for the store, but she'd already looked around only to find places not big enough or with rents too high. Not to mention, the current location was right in the center of town, which was prime real estate for foot traffic.

She leaned back in her chair and looked at the sepia-toned photo of her grandparents that hung on the wall. They stood side-by-side, her grandfather's strong arm around her grandmother's waist. She was smiling so big that her eyes were closed, laughing at something Sadie's grandfather had just said; his face turned to his wife as if whispering in her ear. A private moment someone caught on film that was an accurate depiction of them and their marriage.

All that James had said about his marriage floated into her thoughts. It would be easy to look at that photo of her grandparents and believe they didn't have struggles. Never argued. Sadie had lived with them. She knew better. Not that things were bad, and she'd been a child, so it wasn't as if they argued in front of her. But even with any ups and downs, there wasn't a doubt in her mind her grandparents had loved each other and that they had a good relationship.

Sadie's grandfather would make her grandmother laugh and then look at Sadie and say, "Best sound in the world. I feel ten feet tall when I make her laugh."

Sadie sighed and turned her attention back to the most recent letter from her landlord. She had until the first of the year to make a decision, not nearly enough time to come up with the money to pay down JoJo's medical bills as well as have a plan for increased rent on the store.

Charlie suggested Sadie speak to JoJo. That her aunt was tougher than Sadie was giving her credit for and was the person Sadie needed to make any big decisions with. She didn't regret not telling JoJo up to this point. JoJo did seem to be doing much better, and it would be more jarring for her if Sadie just out of the blue said they had to move. She needed to give JoJo time to process it all, as well as have a vote. Of course, she had a vote. It was her life, too. Sadie had just wanted so much to handle this *for* her aunt, to feel for once as if she was the one taking care of everything for them rather than the other way around. JoJo had been her rock almost her entire life. She just wanted to be that for her in return.

She rubbed her thumb along her bottom lip as she thought about what Charlie had said about gold being buried in Nearlake. It was pretty close to ridiculous to think she'd find any beneath the store, and yet she couldn't subdue the grandiose notion that that could potentially solve all her problems.

Couldn't it?

She shook her head. "Get your head on straight, Woods," she said to the empty room.

It was time to stop chasing fantasies in her head and get to work. She stacked the papers together and shoved them into the desk drawer. They would have to wait until after closing for her to pore over them again, praying an answer would come to her via divine intervention.

Leaving the numbers behind her, she went into the store to check in with Moira and see how things were going with Kenny and Maddie. James had dropped Maddie off earlier, coming inside to say hello and steal a short kiss while no one was looking. He'd also asked her out on a date Friday night. She smiled at the memory, the image of James acting shy when he asked her to dinner. Thinking of James helped her worries float away to a corner of her mind where she could ignore them.

She found Moira behind the main desk wrapping up an order for a customer. Maddie's blond head was bent over a stack of books she had laid out on a table; her focus lasered in on her task. Kenny was diligently rubbing a dresser with a dust rag, his tongue sticking out of his mouth a little, his mind intent on getting every speck of dust from the surface.

Sadie smiled. It was hard to believe that only a few weeks ago, she'd been upset over her window being broken, and there was no one stepping forward to own up to the mistake. Now, Kenny had become a part of the store's family, winning over everyone who worked there, including her.

For a precious moment, she breathed in peace. It would be okay. It had to be.

The bell over the door tinkled, and she looked over to see a short, bald gentleman step through. As the door closed behind him, a whoosh of cold air breezed through, sweeping away with it all the peace she'd had only moments before.

She knew the man. He worked for the company that owned the building.

Before Moira or anyone else saw him, Sadie made her way over and stood before him, if anything, to keep their interaction brief and have him gone before anyone else noticed.

"How may I help you today?" she asked.

"Hello, Miss Woods. I'm from…"

"Yes, I know where you're from."

"Oh. Well." He put a fist to his mouth and coughed. "I am just stopping by to make sure you've received the letters we sent informing you of…"

"Yes. I did. I'm aware of the situation and am figuring things out." She looked behind her, relieved to find Moira still helping a customer and the others going about their work without paying the two of them any attention.

"Okay. Well, good. Just know you have until the first of the year."

"Yes, I know." She forced a smile and gestured toward the door to signal him to leave, which, blessedly, he did.

"Good day, Miss Woods."

As she watched him go down the outside steps, she took in a deep breath and let it out. Her heart raced inside her chest, her awareness that the up and down of her emotions couldn't be good for her.

She made sure he got in his car and drove away before she went back to work. Stopping by to see how Maddie was doing would be a good start.

"How's it going, Maddie?" Sadie asked, hoping her smile looked more genuine than it felt, her heart still pounding against her ribs.

"Great. I've made stacks of the books based on genre, but then some of them have such pretty binding and covers that I'm using those to add as décor around the store."

Sadie's eyes wandered to the rug where the passageway sat beneath. Maddie had left a couple of stacks of books there. The two of them hadn't discussed the passageway since the night Sadie had dinner at James' house. Things had been busy, so it wasn't as if they'd had much opportunity, but Sadie had a feeling James had also made it crystal clear to his daughter not to push the issue after he'd found Sadie down there. Curious as she may be about it, Sadie's stomach turned at the thought of anything bad happening to Maddie, especially if she'd encouraged her.

And yet, she couldn't help but think of what Charlie had said about the buried treasure in Nearlake. Why would the original owners of the building have a hidden passageway beneath if not to keep something secret?

"Sadie?"

Maddie's voice snapped her back to the moment. "Yes."

Maddie's eyes wandered to where Sadie had been staring and then back to her. "I've been thinking about it, too," she whispered. Based on the face she pulled, Sadie was right that James had been adamant with his daughter not to entertain any ideas about what might be down there.

The last thing Sadie wanted was to fuel the fire of her curiosity, so telling Maddie about potential treasure would not be happening.

"I'll admit, it's hard not to," Sadie agreed. She stared longingly again at the spot on the floor as if it might hold the answers to all her problems. She sighed, then focused on Maddie again. "But your dad is right. It's dangerous down there, and until we really know what we are dealing with, it's best to leave it alone."

Although she said the words, believing them was hard, her desire to know what was down there overpowering all rational thought. Maybe after everyone was gone, she'd go again, just for a quick peek.

"Yeah. I guess so." Maddie shrugged. "It's almost time for me to go. My friend and her mom are coming to get me and drive me to her house for dinner and to study for a math test. Is it okay if I leave these stacks here until tomorrow?"

"Absolutely. Good luck with your test." She patted Maddie on the arm. With a chuckle at the eye roll, Maddie threw her way, she went to help Moira start the list of To-Do's it took to close up the shop each night.

Grateful for the distraction of her daily work, Sadie was able to get the shop closed and everyone off for the evening without her mind wandering too often to the stacks of bills awaiting her in the office. But every time she passed the rug covering the trapdoor, she almost felt it calling to her to go back inside. As much as she tried, she couldn't help but hope that maybe Charlie was on to something.

After Moira left and the store was empty, Sadie double-checked that everyone was gone, locked the doors, grabbed a large flashlight behind the main desk, and went over to move the stacks of books Maddie had left on the rug.

Her pulse raced as she wove a story in her head, a tale of robbers needing a place to hide gold, the owners of the shop not knowing, building the passageway to tuck away something valuable to them, not knowing what was truly down there. There could be even more than gold to be discovered.

As she pulled back the rug, she had to laugh at herself. It was clear she'd read too many mystery novels. The grandiose story she'd just concocted was far-fetched, even for fiction.

Or was it?

A loud knock caused her to jump and scream.

She turned to find James standing outside the front window, a look on his face of concern sprinkled with irritation. It was now dusk outside, the sun fading as the few lamps she still had lit in the store began to glow a bit brighter.

She unlocked the door and let him inside.

"You were going to back down there, weren't you?" The tone of his voice did nothing to hide his frustration.

"Well…I just…" Her shoulders sagged, her hope fading. "I just wanted to take a peek."

He rubbed a hand down his face and put his hands on his hips. "You will be the death of me, Woods! You promised you wouldn't go down there again, at least not without me."

Her spirits lifted at that. "You aren't going to tell me not to go down there?"

"Would it make a difference?"

She pursed her lips together to hold back a smile.

"I didn't think so. My best bet is to bite the bullet and go with you." He took off his jacket and laid it across a nearby chair. Sadie knew it was his day off, so he was in jeans and a long-sleeved button-down. He rolled up the sleeves and moved over to the trapdoor together. With a tug at the handle, he lifted the door, the squeak of the hinge echoing through the empty store.

"I go first this time." He grabbed the flashlight she had sitting on a table nearby and flipped the ON switch. "Stay behind me."

She nodded, not trusting her voice or her words. Excitement, curiosity, desperation, and a touch of fear ping-ponged through her system, each emotion vying for top billing. Her stomach turned. She swallowed hard as James made his way down the stairs. She followed behind him, the flashlight he held illuminating the beginning of the tunnel.

Sadie wasn't exactly sure what she expected to see. It wasn't as if gold bars would now be dancing across the lighted tunnel, asking to be found.

James took a few steps, Sadie sticking close to his back. He held the flashlight in one hand, the other curved behind him, holding her close.

"I knew you wanted to come back down here," James

said, "but what made you decide to do so today?"

"Charlie told me that she was reading some local history books and found out there could be gold down here."

With that, James straightened up and turned to her. "Are you serious? It's Idaho. There could be gold buried anywhere."

She looked up at him. "I know that. But what if it's buried *right here*?"

He shook his head and resumed his position, the flashlight pointed forward and Sadie tucked against his back. "And what if it is?"

"Well, I just… Why did you come to the store anyway? I mean, not that I don't want to see you; you just scared me."

"Maddie texted me and said you didn't seem yourself like something was bothering you."

Sadie grimaced inside not hiding her feelings as well as she thought, but was touched that James would come and check on her. Now that they were in the tunnel, she was grateful to not be alone.

They took a few more steps.

"Look up ahead." Sadie pointed around his body. "It looks like there's a door."

They continued.

"Sadie. I don't like this."

James' tone was one Sadie had never heard before.

He'd been scared the first time he found her down there because he thought she was hurt. Now, it sounded as if he was afraid for both of them.

She didn't think it possible, but Sadie's heart raced even faster. She stepped around him and moved toward the door.

His hand reached out and grabbed her arm. "Sadie, wait. We have no idea what's behind there."

"That's why I want to open the door."

His hand held her tight as if he'd lose her if he let go.

She placed a hand over his. "I won't get hurt, James. I need to see…" Desperation began to take the lead of her emotions, her voice raising as she spoke. She pulled her arm away and turned back towards the door.

He moved in front of her. "Fine. But I go in first. We have no clue what's in here."

She didn't know whether to be touched by his chivalry or irritated. From the looks of things, it was a storage cellar. Until that moment, she didn't realize how much her hopes gripped to their being something valuable inside.

A large metal latch held the door closed. James moved the latch, a loud creak echoing as he pushed the door open.

Sadie's heart pounded in her chest as she followed him into the room.

James shined the flashlight around, giving them the chance to see the walls lined with shelves. Sadie moved to one side which held stacks of old newspapers, the paper yellowed with time. Three ink bottles sat nearby, one tipped on its side.

James scuffed his boot along the ground near a cluster of broken glass. He picked up an old bottle off one of the shelves on the opposite side of the room and turned it in his hand.

"These are old booze bottles," he said.

That would explain the glass in the passageway Sadie had cut her hand on. "The building originally held the town newspaper, but why bottles of alcohol?"

"When was it built?" James asked, turning to her.

"1915."

"My best guess is that someone used this for bootlegging during prohibition."

Sadie's mind spun. The history lover in her was geeking out inside at what they'd found, but the hope she'd clung to that they'd find something valuable dimmed and died. The walls of the room began to slowly move in.

James' eyes met hers. "What is it? What's wrong?"

"I need… air."

He put one arm around her and led them back through the passageway, the flashlight in his other hand.

As she climbed the stairs ahead of James, she found it harder and harder to breathe. She mentally berated herself for thinking this could have been her chance to find a way out of her financial mess. What was she thinking? The weight of her reality came crashing down.

She reached the store, tears falling with no way to hold

them back. Her breathing was ragged, her heartbeat pounding in her ears.

James came to her and wrapped an arm around her waist. "Hey. Hey. It's okay. Breathe with me. Slow. Steady."

He took long, deep breaths beside her. She tried to do the same, but it felt as if her lungs had shrunk. Her mind spun with panic, her eyes flowing with tears like a faucet. What was wrong with her? How could she lose control like this?

As if reading her thoughts, James moved in front of her and held her shoulders. "Look at me, Sadie. Look at my eyes."

She had to blink away tears to do so, but she found his eyes. Deep pools of blue. They reminded her of the ocean when JoJo had taken her once to the beach. It was a calm day, the waters playful and welcoming. Sadie had waded in, knowing she'd be safe.

She was safe. James was here. She was safe with James.

He kept his breathing deep and slow and as she focused on his eyes, her breathing beginning to match his, her heart rate slowing down.

"That's it. That's better."

She nodded, her breathing returning to normal.

He swept a stray hair away from her eyes and tucked it behind her ear, then cupped her face in hand, the other still holding her shoulder.

The tender way he held her face and his eyes searching

hers for answers melted away the panic.

"I'm going to lose…" she stuttered between breaths. "I'm going to lose everything."

He pulled her to him and held her close as she cried, with every sob, a piece of her breaking apart inside.

* * *

James held Sadie close, his heart breaking with every sob.

He'd driven immediately to the store when Maddie told him Sadie didn't seem herself. And he was glad he had. He had a sixth sense she was going to go down into that tunnel alone, and the mere thought of it terrified him.

But nothing scared him more than coming out of the cellar and finding her having a full-blown panic attack. No stranger to them himself, as well as helping people through them in his work as a cop, his instincts had kicked in.

Helping others was one thing, but this was Sadie.

Sadie, whose wide brown eyes stared into his, so much fear swimming in them. He'd prayed right then for God to let him carry the weight of her world on his shoulders rather than her.

Seeing her hurting gutted him.

She'd cried in his arms for a while. It didn't matter. She could have done so for hours for all he cared. Holding her was like coming home. Protecting her something he felt born to do.

Once her breathing and sobs subsided, he guided them to one of the sofas in the store.

He tucked her close against him, not wanting to let her go. She sank into his embrace willingly. His own heart rate slowed as he felt her body begin to relax against his.

"I'm sorry."

"You have absolutely nothing to be sorry for, Sadie."

"The rent on the shop is going up. I'm behind on JoJo's medical bills. I fear we'll have to sell the house..." her body moved with small sobs again. "And like an idiot, I had a grand idea this mysterious cellar would hold something valuable to save me. Faith misplaced doesn't even begin to cut it, does it?"

James smiled and placed a kiss on the top of her head. If that didn't show how tenacious the woman was, he wasn't sure what would. So determined to solve things on her own, she risked going into a dark, dangerous tunnel in search of gold.

You couldn't write this stuff.

"I don't know. I think it took quite a bit of faith for you to believe in gold beneath your store."

She swatted his leg with her hand, her body shaking with a small chuckle. "Don't tease me."

"Zero teasing here, ma'am."

She tucked her legs beneath her, settling her head in his

lap.

She fell asleep for a while. James had all night with Maddie at a friend's house, and there was nothing he'd rather do than spend time holding Sadie in his arms. He stroked her head, tucking her hair behind her ear and reveling in the peaceful sound of her breathing.

He knew now more than ever that all he wanted was to take care of her. Be there for her. He only hoped she wanted that as well.

16

JAMES LOOKED AT his watch again. Sadie wasn't late for their date. He was early.

They'd initially planned for him to pick her up, but then something happened at the last minute at the store, and she had to stay longer, so she suggested meeting him at the restaurant.

He took a sip of water and tried to tamp down any doubts he had that she maybe wanted to back out but just didn't want to tell him. No. Sadie wouldn't do that. If she wanted out, she'd say so. He was just nervous. He hadn't been on a date since high school. And back then, going on a date was a whole different thing. Now…well. He folded his hands in front of him on the table and relaxed in his chair.

There was absolutely zero reason to doubt things between him and Sadie. When she'd woken up after sleeping in his lap, she was a little embarrassed. But he had kissed that away; after she'd told him everything that was going on, it was as if the walls she'd had up to protect herself had come down, at least enough for her to trust him, and that meant something. It meant a lot. They'd talked on the phone or texted since, and even in those conversations, he could sense a peace in her that wasn't there before. Her troubles still needed solving, but he had a feeling she found comfort in not carrying them alone.

He understood. It was the exact same way he had felt after he'd told her about Tiffany. Sadie would never share that with anyone, and she would respect his wishes to not let Maddie know the truth about her mother. Someday, when Maddie was a grown woman and could handle it, he would be honest that his relationship with Tiffany had not been healthy. He didn't want Maddie to go into relationships herself with a false sense of idealism. But for now, he found comfort in Sadie knowing, and that was enough.

He looked up as she came through the front door of the restaurant. She stopped to talk to the hostess as if they were old friends. They probably were. James took the opportunity to soak in how beautiful she looked. Her blond hair was swept up into a clip, wisps of curls lining her face. The emerald green dress she wore accentuated her curves, and the flow of the skirt was feminine and soft, just like

Sadie.

She hugged her friend goodbye, and James stood as she came over to the table.

"You are beautiful." He kissed her cheek and then pulled out her chair for her.

"Well, that's a greeting I could get used to," she said as he moved back to the other side of the table and settled into his seat.

"A greeting you deserve every moment of every day." James took great pleasure in how her cheeks flushed with color.

She looked down for a moment, then met his eyes. "This is really nice. I'm so sorry I had to change things and meet here rather than you picking me up."

"It's not a problem. I'm just glad you're here."

Sadie looked around the room. "This is a lovely place. I've only been here a couple of times with JoJo."

"No other date nights here?" It was a loaded question, he knew, but one he didn't regret asking.

She smiled. "I guess not being in our twenties means we can cut to the chase with each other, can't we?"

He laughed. "That wasn't how I meant it, but now that you say it, yeah. I think so. Besides, you now know all my dating history. One woman since high school that ended badly."

She winced. "I think you sell yourself short. There has to be some part of your history with Tiffany that was good."

"There were good times, yes. I don't mean to make it all sound bad."

"You're not. Just honest." She placed her napkin in her lap and took a sip of water. "And you're right. It's only fair that I now share anything from my past. Although I'm sad to say, it will be a short story and a rather boring one at that."

"There's no way I will ever believe you didn't have countless men beating down your door."

He meant it, and yet she laughed hard.

"Believe it, James. I mean, come on. I was the wallflower. In many ways, I still am. I prefer a night at home with a good book over anything social."

"This entire town knows you. You are clearly social."

She lifted a shoulder and let it fall. "That's different. That's just being a good neighbor."

He couldn't fathom how easy it was for her to miss what an amazing person she was, what a treasure she was to her family and her friends. And there was no way she didn't have a trail of men in her past. Mark had said she'd never married and for the life of him, James couldn't imagine why.

As if reading his mind, she said, "As far as dating or marriage, I just never found the right guy. I mean, I guess that's kind of the easy answer. JoJo really wanted me to go away to college to be sure I got out into the world a little before settling in Nearlake. I humored her and went to Boise State. I wouldn't call that 'seeing the world,' but it was as far away from home as I wanted to go. I enjoyed it, but truly just wanted to be home."

The waiter came and took their drink order. When he left, she continued.

"I met a guy in college, and we dated for over a year. We talked about getting married, but when he found out how adamant I was about moving back here, we split up. We just wanted different things."

"And that's it?"

"I told you it was a short and boring story."

"There is no way I can believe that a woman as amazing as you hasn't dated in the past fifteen years."

She laughed. "When you say it that way, I sound like an old spinster who holed up in her house, sworn to stay far away from men."

"Are you?" he teased.

She shook her head, a big smile on her face. "I am not. At least, I don't think I am." She took a sip of her water and set it back down. "It's a small town. I went on a few dates here and there, but my life has become work and community, and now I am taking care of my aunt."

Her smile faded a bit.

"You said it was the two of you most of your life. Has she ever said why she's kept Gary at arm's length all these years?"

Her eyes went wide at that.

"As gorgeous as they are, don't give me those eyes. I

know stuff."

She laughed again, the sound moving through him like a melody he wanted to replay over and over and over again.

"You and Gary are tight, huh?"

"I wouldn't say that. But when I talked to him about fixing the back window of the store, it wasn't hard to see he had feelings for your aunt that went beyond friendship or kindly neighbors." He shrugged. "And I have this uncanny knack for people telling me things when I haven't asked or said a word. They just talk."

"You're trustworthy."

He scoffed at that.

"You are a good man and a trustworthy one, James."

Now, it was his turn to blush. Being around Sadie made him feel young again. All the dark stuff he carried faded into the background with her nearby. All color and light, it was hard for him to imagine not holding her tight and never letting go. That's exactly what James wanted to do. He just needed to know if she wanted that as well.

Their waiter came and took their dinner orders, James opting for a steak while Sadie chose salmon. After he'd taken their menus and walked away, they settled further into their seats.

"Whether others find me trustworthy or not, I just want to say that I'm grateful you trusted me with all you're going through."

She looked down at her lap, her hands toying with her

napkin.

"I know that isn't easy for you. Heck, it's not easy for me, either."

With that, she looked up and met his eyes. "I guess we both tend to think we have to go it alone, don't we?"

He nodded. "I don't think that's how it has to be, though. We can both decide otherwise."

She looked away and then back at him. "My grandparents died when I was nine. My mother left not long after. Barely twenty-one years old, JoJo was mourning her parents, was taking over their store, and had a kid dropped into her lap to raise."

James swallowed hard. He guessed there had to be pain in her background, both parents being out of the picture. However, as a parent, it was hard for him to grasp someone walking away from their child. His heart sank for Sadie and JoJo both.

"Did you know your dad?"

She shook her head. "No. He took off before I was born, which is why my mom moved back to Nearlake. She was a single mother on her own. Once my grandparents died, I think she felt suffocated by responsibility and parenthood. Living in a small town didn't help either, so she left.

"Are you in touch with her now?"

"No. She left and never looked back. JoJo tried to stay connected, but my mom is never in one place at a time. JoJo finally gave up and let her go."

James' gut churned. The last thing he wanted was to judge someone, but he couldn't fathom leaving Maddie, let alone being out in the world, knowing she existed and not wanting any ties to her.

No wonder Sadie thought she had to do everything alone. She'd been abandoned. Loved by her grandparents and her aunt, sure, but with a father who wasn't ever in the picture and a mother who walked away... James' mind and heart couldn't take it all in. Yet again, he wanted to wrap her up in his arms and tell her every moment of every day how much she was loved and valued.

Sadie blinked. "Anyway, I'm sorry. The last thing I wanted to do on a nice evening like this is be a downer." She smiled at him and took a sip of her water.

James shook his head. "Sadie, you are a beautiful soul and the furthest thing from a downer. I'd like nothing more than to sit here for hours and hear your story. I want to know everything about you."

Another rush of color to her cheeks made him smile. If he looked up the word "humble" in the dictionary, he'd find her picture. Along with gracious, kind, generous, the most beautiful woman he'd ever laid eyes on. He'd wax poetic about her forever if she'd let him.

"I want to thank you for being there for me," she said, pulling him from his thoughts. "I'm pleading temporary insanity for even thinking of going down into that passageway alone. I'm grateful you arrived when you did, and although my ego has some things to work through still, I'm also grateful for you listening and…being there for me."

He knew how tough it was for her to say that because it was tough for him to admit the same to her. Although it was easy to trust Sadie and to share his heart with her, it didn't mean it was easy to him to admit it.

"Thank you for trusting me. I'm always here for you."

She smiled.

"Have you thought more about what you might do?"

She took a deep breath in and let it out as if summoning up the courage for what she was going to say. "Yes. I'm going to talk to JoJo. She needs to know anyway, and whatever we decide, we will get through it together like we always have."

"I think that's a good idea."

She nodded. "Me, too."

"I know that will be hard. I'm here…" He reached a hand across the table. She placed hers in his.

"Thank you."

Her phone dinged in her purse.

"I'm so sorry. I only leave that on in case JoJo needs something."

"Don't apologize. Mine is always on for Maddie," he said with an encouraging smile.

She took her phone out of her purse and looked at the screen. All color drained from her face.

"Sadie. Sadie, what is it?"

She looked at him, her eyes wide. "It's JoJo. She's in the ER."

17

THE DOORS OF THE ER made a whoosh sound as Sadie raced through them. James had dropped her off and was parking the car.

Her heart rate had gone through the ceiling when she'd received Moira's text and had maintained that pace the entire drive to the hospital. All Moira's text had said was that JoJo had taken a fall. That she was okay, but Sadie's mind wasn't willing to accept JoJo was fine until she could see for herself. James had quickly paid for the meals they didn't even get to eat, thanked the restaurant staff for understanding, and the two of them had raced out the door. Sadie had tried to continue texting Moira on the way over for more information, but she knew that cell coverage inside the hospital was spotty at best.

The heels of her dress shoes clicked on the tile floor as she made her way to the main desk. With every step, visions of all the visits she and JoJo had already made in the past months flashed through her mind, a collage of snapshots of JoJo in wheelchairs, JoJo with IVs in her arm, the scent of rubbing alcohol and antiseptic making each memory that much more tangible.

She blinked away tears and tried to focus.

"Excuse me," she said to the nurse behind the counter. "My aunt was brought in. Joanna Woods."

The woman looked at her computer screen for a moment. "Yes. She's…"

"Sadie!" Moira came around the corner, her presence cutting into what the nurse was saying.

Sadie hugged her friend, grateful to see her friend. "Moira. How is she?"

Moira pulled back from their embrace and looked at Sadie. "She's fine. Gary is back there with her."

Sadie blinked. Gary? Why would Gary be with JoJo?

One side of Moira's mouth twitched up for a brief second as if in on a secret but wasn't going to share.

Sadie shook her head. She'd come back to those thoughts in a moment. Right now, she needed to know what had happened to JoJo.

James came up behind her and placed a hand on her back. "Any news? What happened?"

"She's fine." Moira placed a hand on Sadie's arm. "She tripped over something in her quilting room and landed on her wrist. It's broken, but they are getting it set and putting a cast on it right now. She'll be fine."

Relief flooded Sadie's system at the same time her mind raced over her aunt being alone and hurt without her there to help. And with all that JoJo had been through, it turned Sadie's stomach. JoJo now had one more thing that needed healing.

"You can go back and see her," Moira said. "There can only be two of us at a time, so I came out to find you and tell you to go see her."

James wrapped his arm around Sadie's waist and gave a gentle squeeze with his hand. "You go. I'll wait here." He gave her a kiss on the side of her head.

Moira's eyebrows lifted as she looked at Sadie, then turned her attention to James. "I'll join you." She stepped to James' other side and slipped a hand through his arm. "Come on. I know which coffee makers are the best ones. We can find a cup and sit and chat."

Sadie's eyes met James'. She gave him a soft nod to assure him she was okay. He squeezed her side again, then slowly let go as if it was difficult for him to do so. However, with Moira on his other side urging him towards coffee, he didn't have much choice.

As James and Moira made their way down the hall, the nurse behind the counter stood and said, "I'll take you back there."

"Thank you."

Sadie followed the woman through a set of double doors down a hallway lined with small rooms with gurneys inside and barely enough space for someone to move around from one side to the other.

"She's right in here."

"Thank you," Sadie said again as the woman nodded and went back to her post.

The door was cracked a little, and Sadie peeked inside. JoJo was propped up in the bed, an IV drip in her arm, and her wrist propped in her lap and wrapped heavily. Sadie stepped back for a moment, her breath catching, tears threatening to fall. Seeing JoJo in a hospital bed again caused all of Sadie's fears and worries to rush over her like a tidal wave. The rational part of her brain that said all that had happened was a broken wrist couldn't overpower the emotions that still came when she thought about losing her aunt. The only family she had left and the one person she'd relied on her entire life.

There was no way she could tell JoJo now about their financial problems. How could she possibly move JoJo out of the house or even suggest the possibility? Her thoughts raced at the same pace as her heart.

She peered in again and saw Gary sitting at JoJo's bedside, his hand holding JoJo's uninjured one in his.

Sadie's head tilted. What was that about? She knew

JoJo and Gary were friends, but by the look in Gary's eyes and the level of concern on his face, was there more to their relationship?

She knocked lightly on the door, then poked her head inside before stepping into the room.

JoJo looked at her; her eyes were rimmed with moisture, and she had a small smile on her face.

Was Gary making her cry? What was going on?

"Sadie! Oh, my goodness. Come in," her aunt said.

JoJo didn't sound upset. She sounded…happy.

Gary stood. He let go of JoJo's hand then shoved his into the pockets of his jeans "Hi, Sadie. He gave her a small smile.

"Hi, Gary."

It could have been the lighting in the room, but she could swear it looked as if the rims of Gary's eyes were red from crying.

"I'll leave you two alone," he said. With a wink and nod toward JoJo, he moved around the bed and out the door.

Sadie watching him go, a list of questions forming in her head. Questions she would push to the back of her mind for now, her attention turning to her aunt.

"JoJo. I can't believe this happened." She moved around to where Gary had been sitting and took his place in the chair at her aunt's bedside.

"Oh, it was just an accident." It wasn't new for JoJo to brush things off as not a big deal. Never wanting attention, she tended to act as if she could carry the weight of the world on her own. In Sadie's mind, JoJo had done that very thing for most of her life.

JoJo was so vulnerable and had been so for months now. How could Sadie have let her guard down and focused on herself so much? Her heart ached at the thought of James' support, the small touches in the hospital hallway that spoke volumes of how he was right there for her. How Sadie felt so safe in his arms, so adored every time he looked at her.

She wanted that. She wanted all of it. And yet, at what cost?

Right in front of her was proof of how vulnerable JoJo was and how much she still needed her. And where had Sadie been? On a date with James.

"I can almost see the smoke coming from your brain," JoJo said, interrupting Sadie's thoughts. "You keep thinking like that, and you'll hurt yourself."

Sadie pulled a face.

"Don't look at me like that," JoJo admonished, a note of teasing in her voice.

"JoJo. You're lying in a hospital bed."

"You have a firm grasp of the obvious, Loves. And I am here because it was an accident. I got dehydrated and a little lightheaded. I stood up from my sewing table and…well, the rest is right here," she said as she pointed to her wrapped wrist.

"Why didn't you call me?"

"I didn't want to interrupt your date."

Sadie shook her head.

"I called Gary, and he came right over and brought me here. It's all fine."

It didn't feel all fine. Sadie feared things might never feel fine ever again.

"You look so lovely," JoJo smiled at her.

Sadie looked down at her dress. She'd all but forgotten she'd taken the time to do her hair special and dress up for the evening, the events that unfolded becoming all she could focus on. Sitting with James at the restaurant felt like a distant memory even thought it had been a mere hour or so ago.

However, the conversation with James was at the forefront of her thoughts. She'd decided to tell JoJo everything, but now? Now Sadie's feelings had dropped right back to where she'd been, the sense of dread weighing her down. How could she solve their financial issues without turning JoJo's world, or her own, upside down?

JoJo reached out her hand. Sadie leaned forward, resting her arms on the side of the bed, her hands holding JoJo's.

"Talk to me, Loves."

Sadie's shoulders sagged. Tears threatened to fall, and out of sheer exhaustion, she let them.

JoJo squeezed her hand and said nothing, just gave

Sadie the gift of her presence as she cried, her forehead resting on the side of JoJo's bed, her hands holding onto her aunt's as if the only lifeline she had.

After a few minutes, JoJo said, "I think it's time we talk, Sadie."

Sadie looked up. JoJo only called her Sadie when she was serious.

"I know what you've been carrying alone, and it's time you let me in on it. On everything."

Sadie sat up in her chair and gently took her hands from JoJo's so she could grab a tissue from a nearby box and wipe her face. JoJo was a mother to Sadie, and her voice held a tone she only used when speaking to her. "What do you mean?"

"I know about the rent being raised, and I know that we're stretched because of medical bills."

Sadie's shoulders sagged again. She couldn't decide if she was relieved JoJo knew or irritated with herself that she hadn't hidden it all as well as she would have liked.

As if reading her mind, JoJo said, "You hid it pretty well, I'll give you that, but based on clues I sniffed out from knowing you so well, along with Moira having a gut feeling of what was going on, we pieced it together. Not to mention, you aren't quite as good at hiding paperwork as you think."

Sadie frowned.

"Moira is our right hand at the store, Sadie. She has to

go through the desk and paperwork from time to time."

Sadie sat back in the chair, her hands now in her lap toying with the tissue.

"I don't know what to do," Sadie said, the tears once more sliding down her cheeks.

"Oh, Loves." JoJo reached her hand out again, and Sadie leaned forward to hold it in her own.

"I don't have a lot of regrets in this life, but I do regret teaching you that we are to do this life alone. That everything we carry would only be a burden to others if we reach out for help."

Sadie sat up and leaned closer to her aunt. "That's not true, Jo. You are the most generous, giving person I know."

"Well, thank you for saying that, but that is giving. I'm terrible at receiving."

Sadie let that soak in, James' words at dinner coming to mind. It's not even about asking for help with physical things like fixing a broken garbage disposal or bathroom sink. The toughest burdens to share with others were emotional. That takes trust.

"I'm sorry I didn't trust you with everything," Sadie admitted. "I thought I was protecting you. I just didn't want to put anything else on your plate while you were in treatment and healing."

"You were being thoughtful, and I appreciate that."

"But from now on it will be you and me against the world again." She meant the words but as she said them, the desire to be with James tugged at her heart, the sense that she had to choose one over the other causing her emotions to wrestle inside of her.

"That's another thing I regret," JoJo said with a frown. "I regret I may have taught you not to give love a chance. That it wouldn't be worth it or, God forbid, that it would mean one of us was abandoning the other."

Sadie's stomach turned.

"I want to tell you something." JoJo's eyes met Sadie's. "You asked me not too long ago if I had jumped into anything when I was younger, and I told you that I had thought about it but didn't. That I was fine with my feet planted firmly where they were."

Sadie nodded, recalling the conversation.

JoJo took a deep breath in and let it out. "I was in love years ago."

Whatever Sadie expected JoJo to say, that wasn't it.

"You were about ten years old. It wasn't long after my parents died and your mother left. I was young and had a lot on my plate at once." She squeezed Sadie's hand. "Don't get me wrong. I was happy, just overwhelmed. Theo and I started dating, and he was wonderful. Kind. Caring. He was everything I thought I wanted."

Sadie tried to flip through the files of her brain to recall anything about Sadie dating. She couldn't remember any men in JoJo's life other than Gary, to be honest. Certainly, no one took JoJo out on dates or came over to the house.

"He knew all about you and our situation, but I kept him at length, not wanting you to get too attached or close to him in case we broke up. Which is what we did."

"Was it a relationship with him the thing you didn't jump at back then, Jo?"

She nodded. "We cared a great deal for each other, but he wanted to move around, see the world. Nearlake wasn't for him." She shrugged. "It wasn't even Nearlake, really. He liked it here. But he wanted to travel a ton, possibly live in different places for months at a time. And I didn't want that."

Sadie's heart sank in her chest. She had always felt a sense of guilt over all that JoJo had given up to raise her. Until now, she didn't know just how much that was. "I'm so sorry, Jo." She shook her head. "Raising me cost you so much."

"Now, you just wait a minute. That is nonsense. And that is not why I am telling you this." She squeezed Sadie's hand tighter. "I am telling you I made my choice, and I don't regret that for a second. I love this place. It's my home. I love the store. It's my life's work and the legacy my parents left for us. And you, Sadie, are the greatest gift God could have ever given me. Raising you was the greatest joy of my life. The relationship we have now is just the cherry on the sundae. And the truth is, Theo was a wonderful man. But we weren't right for each other. We wanted so many different things. It was a tough decision, but it was the right one."

Gary's voice echoed into the room from the hallway. He was outside the door talking with one of the nurses.

JoJo smiled and looked from the door to Sadie. "I'm telling you all of this, Loves, because what I regret is teaching you that love isn't worth the risk. I blocked love after that. And I don't want to do that anymore. I waited way too long, and the last thing I want for you is to do the same. Don't make the same mistake as me, Sadie. If you have found love, grab hold with both hands and don't let go."

18

"YOU REALLY LOVER her, don't you?"

James stopped pacing and looked at Moira.

"Yes, I do."

It had only been about thirty minutes since Sadie had gone back into the emergency room to visit with her aunt, yet to James, it felt like a lifetime. The coffee Moira had gotten for him sat on a small table in the waiting room, cold and untouched. His stomach wasn't up for it. While a mere short time ago, he was looking across the table at the restaurant, eager to share a good meal while listening to Sadie laugh about her dating history and then share her family story, his insides now churned.

He felt helpless. And he hated that feeling.

He put his hands in his pockets and looked at Moira. She'd asked the question, and he'd given a response without hesitation.

He loved Sadie. It felt a little off to be telling that to Moira before ever saying it to Sadie, but he realized he'd tell the whole world if he could, put up a billboard downtown even.

Moira smiled. "You two are good together." "What makes you say that?"

She set her coffee cup down on the table next to his. She was sitting in a chair, relaxed, as if hospital visits were the norm. Maybe for her, they were. Sadie had told him Moira and JoJo had been friends for a long time. He was sure that meant Moira had walked the road of her illness with her.

Moira set her elbows on the arms of the chair and looked up at him. "I've known Sadie most of her life. She's loyal to a fault. And yet she's trained herself to only get so close to people—then if they leave, her heart is spared."

James nodded. That made sense, especially after all Sadie had told him at dinner.

"Jo decided to just forgo letting a man in, mainly because life had tossed so much at her that she convinced herself she was too busy for it. Sadie was abandoned and has only felt safe with Jo." She leaned forward and placed her elbows on her knees. "I think you're good for her because there is not a doubt in my mind that you would never leave her."

His mouth curved into a glimpse of a smile. "That's true."

Moira smiled. "I can see it in how you look at her. How you pay attention to the little things." She leaned back in her chair again with a chuckle. "Sadie thinks I'm oblivious, but it's hard to work in the shop with her almost every day and not see or hear things." She nodded. "You two are good together."

James nodded again, an unspoken thank you.

Moira was right. And Sadie was good for him, too. He wasn't even aware of how much he needed to relax until he was around her and let go of all the emotions he tried to keep clenched in his fists.

After Tiffany died, James had put his head down, focusing on work and being a good dad to Maddie. Loving someone again was the furthest thing from his mind. But maybe there was some truth to what his brother had said. Maybe he'd spent so much time thinking it wasn't okay to want something for himself that he'd started to believe it.

Then, the call had come in from Sadie's shop. He'd taken one look at her frozen in place, determined not to hinder an investigation and from that point on his life, not to mention his heart, had been turned around in the best ways possible.

He sensed Sadie was there before he turned and saw her in the doorway of the waiting room. Her eyes were red from crying, her makeup blotchy from where she'd wiped her face. She was the most beautiful thing he'd ever seen.

"How is she?" he asked.

"She's fine. It's just her wrist. Gary is with her now and will bring her home later when they release her."

Moira stood and came over to Sadie and hugged her. "She's in good hands," Moira said as she pulled back and looked at Sadie. "I'm gonna head home, but I'll see you tomorrow." She turned and looked at James, then back to Sadie. "You're in good hands, too." With a smile and pat on James' arm, she left the room.

"I'm so sorry about our date, James."

He closed the gap between them and pulled her to him, wrapping her up in his arms as answer. Her body relaxed in his embrace and right then he decided he'd fight to the death to do what was necessary to hold her forever.

He kissed her on the top of the head. "Let's get you home."

* * *

James guided his truck through town. The radio was on, Tracy Chapman singing *Stand By Me*. Sadie laid her head back against the passenger seat and soaked in the peaceful sound of one of her favorite singers as well as a favorite song.

The evening's events ran through her mind; the entire night was a perfect depiction of her life.

Don't relax for too long, Woods. The other shoe will *drop.*

She shook her head. Was she really so far down the path of hopelessness that she couldn't see the good in anything anymore?

The song spoke of the moonlight being all that shines in the dark, but wasn't that enough? Any light in darkness was cause for hope, wasn't it?

JoJo had admitted she knew of the financial trouble they were in, but they didn't get a chance to talk about a solution. Gary had come back into the room, and in all honesty, Sadie's mind was filled with all that JoJo had told her, trying to wrap her head around it. It shouldn't surprise her that her aunt had been in love and even considered marriage, and she wanted to believe what JoJo said about the decision not being about Sadie, but how could that be one hundred percent true? If she hadn't been given Sadie to raise, would she have considered traveling the world with Theo?

They pulled into her drive and James came around and opened her door for her, gave her his hand to help her out of the truck and didn't let go as they walked to her front door. He'd been quiet the whole drive, sensing she wasn't ready to talk. Their date had been railroaded by a visit to the emergency room and he had done nothing but support her.

Just like the song, he stood by her.

They went inside, Sadie flipping on lights as she went, slipping off her shoes and letting them fall in the front hallway. James closed the door behind them and followed her into the family room.

"How about I make us some coffee?" he asked.

"I would love a cup of tea, actually," she said.

He nodded. "Tea it is."

She folded the blanket that lay across JoJo's chair and placed it across the arm so Jo could grab it easily once Sadie got her settled. The clink of pottery mixed with the sounds of James opening and closing cupboards came from the kitchen. Sadie took a deep breath in and let it out. Not a single problem in her life had been solved. In fact, there were more things to worry about with JoJo's injured wrist. And yet, the sound of James moving around her house, being there and making her tea, eased her heart. She turned and sat down hard on the sofa and placed her head in her hands.

The tears came freely, and she let them.

By the time James came and sat beside her, a mug of hot tea placed before her on the coffee table, the skirt of her dress was damp, and her eyes felt like small slits in her face. He put an arm around her and pulled her to him.

How this man was still around, she had no clue. Since walking into her life things had been nothing but chaos, drama, and her crying more than she'd cried in years.

She had no idea how long they sat there that way. Once she'd calmed down, he reached for the mug and handed it to her, along with a tissue he pulled from his shirt pocket.

"A man who's prepared," she teased through her tears.

"I have a teenage daughter."

Sadie coughed out a laugh. "Fair enough."

"Do you want to talk about anything? If not, I understand. I'm happy to sit here and hold you for as long as you need."

The man was a saint.

She smiled and turned, tucking one leg under her so she could face him. He shifted as well. "JoJo is fine. I mean, she did break her wrist, and I feel a huge sense of guilt over not being here with her but…" she stared down into her tea that was cradled in both hands before taking a sip.

"She's gonna be okay," he said as he tucked a lock of hair behind her ear.

The tenderness of his touch sent a wave of peace through Sadie.

She nodded. Yes, JoJo would be okay. But would she?

"You're gonna be okay, too," he said, reading her thoughts.

She leaned forward to set her mug down on the table, then relaxed her shoulder against the back of the couch.

James had an arm across the back, his hand now resting on her shoulder. "JoJo knows. In fact, she already knew about the money troubles."

James nodded as if that fact didn't surprise him. It shouldn't have surprised Sadie, either, really. She'd been so mentally wrapped up in all of it that she'd forgotten how connected her aunt was. It wasn't as if JoJo was sitting here at home, totally reclusive and not communicating with anyone. Apparently, Gary was visiting her more than Sadie knew, and of course, Moira kept her abreast of all the comings and goings of the town. Why would that keep Jo from knowing what was going on under her own roof? Sadie had to chuckle at it all. She was a fool to think she'd been handling anything by herself.

Of course, there still were no answers for what was next. Fear crept in again, turning her stomach. Even though JoJo shared the story of what had happened in her past and the two of them now faced the future together, no solid plan had been established.

Tears formed in Sadie's eyes again.

"Talk to me," James said, his hand rubbing her shoulder.

"I still can't fight the fear I'm going to lose everything. JoJo. The store. Everything I've ever known. Everything I've ever cared about."

"JoJo is fine. She's doing well after her radiation treatments, and I have a feeling a broken wrist won't slow her down. And you will figure out the store. You're not alone, Sadie. Not anymore."

Something in her heart stirred at his words, yet she still couldn't fight the instinct to go it alone.

"I need to be here for her. What if something happens and she's alone? She falls again, and I'm not here." She shook her head. "She has always been there for me. The last thing I want is to be selfish, to want anything beyond being there for her."

"Wanting something for yourself isn't selfish, Sadie." He scoffed. "Believe me, that's something I've only recently learned myself. And you and JoJo aren't alone. Gary was here the minute she called for help. Moira beat us to the hospital."

Sadie looked down, her hands in her lap, toying with the skirt of her dress.

"I'm scared, James."

Scared of her feelings. Scared of loving him. Scared of what that meant and the risk of heartache involved.

"I'm scared, too, Sadie. Well, I was."

She looked at him. He tucked her hair behind her ear again, then ran his fingers gently across her cheek. "Moira asked me tonight at the hospital if I loved you." He smiled. "Without hesitation, I said yes. I love you, Sadie. On paper, it looks like we've only known each other for a short while, but I feel you've known me forever. You see in me things I don't even see myself half the time. You calm me. Whenever I hold you, it's like I'm home."

He cupped her cheek, and she leaned into his touch.

"And I still see that curious, intuitive girl I knew in high school. But it hasn't taken long to see the strong, independent, fiercely loving woman you are now. You would do anything for the people you love."

She shook her head. "That's just it, James. Part of what scares me is that I don't know how to love." She shrugged. "I've never really been in love."

"You have a greater understanding of love than anyone I've ever seen, Sadie."

Her eyes searched his for meaning.

"You love your aunt, this community. Love is the solid foundation of the life you've built here."

"It's only been me and Jo. I've never let anyone in. You're the first person I've allowed to get close enough to…hurt if you left."

"That won't happen, Sadie."

"You can't promise me that, James."

He shifted his body on the sofa so he was facing her completely. He held her face in his hands, assuring she met his eyes. "Sadie. You're right. I can't promise that God won't take me home tomorrow. I know JoJo's illness has you thinking about her dying. You lost your grandparents. The people you love leave or die. That's been your past. But I can promise you that your future can be me loving you every minute of every day God allows me breath on this earth."

He leaned forward, placing a soft kiss on her lips, then rested his forehead on hers. "I love you so much, Sadie Woods. Please trust me with your heart. Please let me love you."

Sadie melted into his touch, tears now rolling down her cheeks. With every word James spoke, the walls around her heart began to fall. Her mother's abandonment may have been the first bricks, but over time Sadie had added to it, not allowing love into her life. Yes, she and JoJo had friends and a community, but at arms' length.

JoJo's words came to Sadie's mind.

"If you have found love, grab it with both hands and don't let go."

"I know it's scary, Sadie. I know. But the thought of life without you in it scares me more than the risk involved in taking a leap of faith that we were meant to be together."

She tried to imagine life before James had come through her door before she'd spent time laughing with Maddie and getting to know her. She couldn't. It was as if her world was blurry before they came along and brought clarity and color.

It was time. It was time to do what JoJo said, to grab hold of the love Sadie had found and not let go.

"I love you, too, James."

His face lit up with a wide smile. His arms wrapped around her waist, and he pulled her to him. Up against him, she soaked in the warmth and comfort of his embrace. She'd found love, and she was ready to hold it tight and not let go.

19

NO MATTER HOW hard Sadie wanted time to stop or even slow down, the holiday season didn't want to cooperate. Thanksgiving came in a blink, whether her life was ready for it or not.

After that night in the hospital, JoJo and Sadie had settled into their same routine, although it was altered a bit by JoJo only having one working hand. With her wrist in a cast, it meant that she needed more help with daily tasks, and even though it pained her to do so, JoJo was getting better at not only asking for help, but also accepting it.

Between Gary, Moira, James, and Sadie, they were able to check in each day and make sure JoJo was cared for; plus, Jan and Evan from next door stopped by almost daily.

And Maddie now spent a day or two a week learning how to quilt and sew from JoJo. Sadie could see that having Maddie around boosted JoJo's spirits. She was recovering well now the radiation was done and her wrist was more of a nuisance than anything else. Not that JoJo would ever complain if she were in pain, but she took her meds without fail and rested and did what was prescribed for her to heal.

James was right. They weren't alone.

And Thanksgiving was Sadie's favorite holiday. This year, she and JoJo were invited to Charlie's house for the day. James and Maddie were joining. His parents were on a cruise for the week, and his brother's family was going to spend the holiday with his in-laws. Charlie's son, Eli, would be home, but not her daughter. She and her boyfriend were spending the day with his family in Boise. Anne had left not long after their lunch together. She was vague about when she'd return but promised she wouldn't be gone as long as before. Charlie was making the turkey, and the rest of them each brought a side dish.

Sadie was putting the finishing touches on the sweet potatoes when JoJo came into the kitchen. Her favorite part of the dish was placing the small marshmallows all around the top, the design melting into a gooey, yummy addition to the meal.

"Those smell and look delicious," JoJo said as she popped a marshmallow into her mouth.

Sadie smiled as she watched her aunt. Her eyes were brighter every day, and her cheeks had color. Earlier that week, they'd heard from the doctor that all signs of JoJo's cancer were gone. A miracle Sadie thanked God for every minute of every day since receiving the word.

"I wondered if you and I could talk for a minute before we head over to Charlie's house?" JoJo asked.

Sadie searched her aunt's face for signs of something wrong and found none. In fact, the woman almost glowed. Sadie hoped that one day soon, she would learn how to think positive thoughts before negative ones, but with the year they'd had, it took some doing and a lot of prayer on her part. But she was getting there. Seeing JoJo improve every day, as well as having James and Maddie as a part of her daily existence, was helping her heart shift from fear to hope.

"Sure." Sadie placed the last of the marshmallows on the potatoes and then washed her hands. "What's up?"

"Let's go sit in the family room."

The two women settled into their spots, JoJo in her chair and Sadie on the sofa.

"I have some news, and I wanted to tell you first before anyone else," JoJo said, leaning forward in her chair.

Sadie's gut clenched. The last time they discussed any news, it was about JoJo's diagnosis.

Reading Sadie's facial expression JoJo reached out a hand and put it on Sadie's knee. "Don't worry, Loves. It's all good. Great, really."

Was her aunt blushing? Now Sadie was really confused.

JoJo sat up tall, took a deep breath, and let it out. "Gary asked me to marry him. And I said yes."

Sadie's eyes went wide.

"Oh, don't look so surprised." JoJo batted Sadie's leg.

"Surprised? I'm shocked!"

"Stop. You've always known how he feels about me."

"I'm not shocked he asked. I'm shocked you said yes!"

Both women laughed.

"Okay. I'll give you that," JoJo said.

"Jo! I am so happy for you!" Sadie leaned forward and hugged her aunt.

Her emotions felt as if she had just ridden the Tilt-A-Whirl at the county fair. From the fear that JoJo had bad news to shock at Gary's proposal, her mind now raced with what that meant for her and JoJo moving forward; she was a tornado of thoughts and feelings.

"When did this happen?" Sadie asked as they settled back into their seats again.

"In the hospital. Gary said he realized it wasn't the romantic way to do it, but he didn't want to waste another minute. The two of us have been dancing around this for far too long."

"I agree with that."

JoJo scrunched up her face. "I'll admit it was more my stubbornness than Gary's that has kept us from being together all this time, but that's what I was trying to tell you in the hospital. Don't wait, Sadie. I went far too long, not allowing myself to love Gary or let him love me. And I'm so glad you took my advice. You and James are perfect for one another."

"I think so, too," Sadie agreed. "But Jo, that was three weeks ago. Why are you only telling me this now?"

JoJo lifted a shoulder and let it fall. "I wanted some time to hold the news close, have it to myself. And Gary and I had a few things we wanted to work out before we told you."

Sadie furrowed her brow. "What kinds of things?"

"Well, the main one is the house. I know you and I discussed selling it to pay off medical costs and help with the raise in rent, but Gary didn't want me to give up my home. So, he'd like to move in here with me. He's lived a bachelor's life in a small apartment for years. Between his savings and what he makes at his shop, we would have enough to cover the mortgage, and that's what he wants. What we want."

Sadie could only imagine how hard it would be for Jo to accept Gary helping her financially. Based on the look on JoJo's face, she could also imagine how being loved by Gary softened Jo's stubbornness to accept the situation.

"He says he has nothing to spend his money on otherwise." JoJo laughed. "The simplicity of that man is one of the things I love about him."

Sadie's heart filled seeing JoJo so happy. And what a gift for Gary to want live with Jo and help her pay the bills.

"And we both want you to know you have a home here with us for as long as you want it."

Wrapped up in the joy of the moment, she hadn't thought about what it would mean for her to have Gary move in. And although she appreciated their kindness, saying she could stay, she couldn't imagine being a third wheel to them after they married.

"That last thing I would want to do is cramp your style, Jo. You and Gary will be newlyweds. You won't want me rattling around here with you."

She meant the words and yet her mind spun a bit over the fact that she now would be looking for a new place to live. She mentally chuckled. If that wasn't life though. Get one issue solved and another pops up.

But today was about focusing on all she was thankful for and with JoJo being cancer free, marrying Gary, and being happier than Sadie had seen her in a long time, there was much to be thankful for. Not to mention James and Maddie and all of her friends she would be celebrating with.

"Well, just know that you are welcome to stay as long as you'd like." JoJo put her hand once more on Sadie's knee. "And I want you to know and believe that me allowing Gary into my life and heart changes nothing between you and me. I love you so much, child. You are my heart. You are my daughter in every way. Nothing and no one can ever change that."

Sadie leaned forward to hug her aunt. "I do know, and I do believe you."

They let go, each of them wiping tears from their eyes, Sadie grateful that this time they were tears of joy.

"Let's get the food wrapped up and get going," JoJo said as she slapped her leg with her good hand and stood. "We have a celebration to get to."

"Yes, we do."

As Sadie put a top on the potatoes and prepared to leave, she smiled at the fact that JoJo was the only mother she needed. And it would always be them against the world, no matter who came into their lives. That only meant they'd be stronger. More love meant more of…everything. She popped a marshmallow into her mouth.

All the good stuff and more.

* * *

While Sadie wouldn't be inclined to call Thanksgiving dinner a party, that's exactly what it was at Davis and Charlie's house. Their home was a large estate, really, outside of town. With Davis' family being one of the founding families of Nearlake, his grandfather had made sure some of the historic homes stayed in the family, therefore guaranteeing their legacy would be preserved.

Sadie loved it.

On ten acres with plush fir trees and lots of space, the house itself was a Victorian design, complete with a wraparound porch and large columns, giving it a grand stature. Because of Charlie and the light, yellow paint she'd chosen, as well as flowers and greenery all around the house, although grand, it was warm and welcoming.

Gary and JoJo had shared their news over dinner and the group had toasted the happy couple. Sadie's heart couldn't help but fill with warmth over JoJo's happiness. She wasn't sure she'd ever seen Gary smile that big, either. Everyone was overjoyed for them.

It had snowed a few days before, but the sun was out, and the weather was close to fall perfection. And what Thanksgiving Day wouldn't be complete without a touch football game? It was evening, the meal eaten and cleaned up, naps having been taken by the men, their energy now revived.

Sadie, Charlie, and JoJo all sat on the porch sipping tea and watching the others play football in the yard. Hesitant at first to play with a former NFL wide receiver, Gary and Davis teased James about going easy on them, which he did. Sadie loved seeing how relaxed he was, laughing with Davis and teaching Eli a thing or two about the game.

"I think it's safe to say this is my favorite Thanksgiving ever," JoJo said, then sipped her tea.

Sadie had to agree. It was the most peaceful she'd felt in a long time. She stole a glance at Charlie, who smiled, but it didn't reach her eyes. Sadie knew it was hard for Charlie not to have Gabby with them for the holiday. Accepting that your kids had adult lives was easier said than done. Or so Charlie had said.

Maddie squealed as James grabbed her around the waist and spun her around, the football tucked firmly in Maddie's arms. With her back tucked up tight against her dad, she kicked out her feet and laughed.

Maddie had only been in Sadie's life a short time, but her heart already ached at the thought that one day, she would watch Maddie drive off to navigate her own journey. What Charlie was feeling must be so much more in-depth than that.

Davis broke away from the group and climbed the porch steps to where they were. "Any chance we can grab more pie?" He wiggled his eyebrows at Charlie, who laughed.

"Of course. But I think there are only about four pies left, so pace yourself."

Davis patted his stomach. "I'm no rookie, babe," he said as he winked at Charlie, then turned to the others in the yard. "Anyone else want more pie?"

A chorus of yeses was the reply.

The group began to make their way inside. As Sadie stood to follow everyone in, James slipped his hand into hers. "Can I talk to you for a second?"

Sadie set her tea mug down on a nearby table. "Of course."

James led her to a corner of the porch and then turned, taking both her hands in his. Where he'd been relaxed a moment ago playing football, he now looked almost nervous.

"Sadie, I'm not even sure I knew what love looked like until I met you. Not long ago, you said you feared you didn't know how to love. But the way you love Jojo, your friends, the way you love Maddie and me. All of it is the purest depiction of love I've ever seen or known."

With his hands still firmly grasping hers, he got down on one knee. Out of his pocket, he pulled out a small box and opened it. An oval diamond in an antique setting sparkled against the black velvet.

Tears ran down Sadie's cheeks, her smile wide.

"I love you, Sadie. Would you marry me? Let me love you for life?"

"Yes!"

He stood and scooped her up in his arms.

A window nearby squeaked as it opened. "Did she say yes?" Maddie asked through the screen.

James set Sadie down but kept her wrapped in his arms. "She did."

A chorus of shouts and "woohoo's" floated out the window.

"Maddie knew?" Sadie smiled up at James.

"Maddie knew. To be honest, she's been bugging me to ask you. She kept coming up with all these grandiose ways to do it."

They both laughed. "And you chose a quiet corner of Charlie's porch?"

"I did. I chose a time when you're surrounded by those you love and who love you."

"Thank you. It's perfect." She looked at the house and then back to him. "So, Maddie's okay with this?"

"She's over the moon." He cupped her face in his hands. "And so am I. I love you so much, Sadie Woods."

"Soon to be Sadie Larsen," she teased.

James smiled. "I love the sound of that."

"I love you, James."

His lips met hers, and her world was complete.

She was home.

EPILOGUE

SADIE STOOD IN a corner of Charlie's living room and looked around. It felt as if the entire town was jammed into the house. Michael Bublé crooned from the speakers installed in the ceiling about how it was beginning to look like Christmas, and based on the enormous tree in the corner, as well as garland everywhere and twinkle lights on anything that stood still, Christmas had definitely found the Benson household.

"What are you doing here all by yourself?" Charlie asked as she handed Sadie a mug of hot chocolate. "I'm having high school flashbacks of you as a wallflower."

Sadie shook her head. "That can't be right because you have to actually *go* to parties to be a wallflower. I was usually at home curled up with a book."

Charlie shrugged and then took a sip from her own mug. "True. But I'm glad to find a moment with you."

"Oh yeah? What's up?"

"I want to give you your Christmas present."

"Now?" Sadie looked around at all the groups of people chatting and laughing. Yule tide cheer was in abundance, yet it hardly seemed the time for her and Charlie to exchange Christmas gifts.

"Yes. Now." Charlie set her mug down and faced Sadie. "We have been friends for a very long time. And I know how hard it is for you to accept help from others as well as believe just how much you mean to this community. After you told me and Anne what was going on with the store, we started a fund online letting everyone in town know that you and JoJo could use some help. As of today, this lovely group of people," she waved her hand across the room, "has raised enough to pay off JoJo's medical bills."

Sadie's mouth dropped open.

"Sadie, you and JoJo mean so much to so many people. As soon as it was known you needed a little help, people stepped up. That's what we do around here. You are loved."

Sadie set down her mug and wiped away tears that threatened to fall. "I don't know what to say."

"Say thank you." Charlie hugged her and then pulled back. "And Merry Christmas."

"Merry Christmas!" Sadie pulled Charlie in for another hug and held her tight.

When they let go, Charlie said, "Now, stop being a wallflower and enjoy your own wedding celebration!"

She grabbed her mug and left to join James, who was talking to Davis.

"Hey, you two," she said as James placed a kiss on her cheek and wrapped an arm around her.

"Sadie!" Davis said as he sat down his champagne glass on a nearby table then rubbed his hands together. "I wanted to talk to you. I was just telling James that Charlie told me about the cellar under your store. My family owned that building from the 1940s through the 1970s. I went through our company's archives and found the blueprints."

"No way!" Sadie looked at James and then back at Davis.

"The cellar is on there and was originally storage for the newspaper, but based on what James said you guys found, I think he's right. It was probably used at some point for bootlegging during prohibition."

Sadie shook her head. "That is so crazy. All that time it's been down there."

"Your grandparents never mentioned it?" Davis asked.

"No. I asked JoJo, and she thinks they would have seen it when they first moved in but probably covered it up to keep me from finding it, the curious kid that I was."

"That trait has not left you, my love," James said, then kissed her forehead.

Davis smiled, "Well, I just wanted you to know. I'm sorry you didn't find gold. That would have been amazing."

Sadie swatted James on the chest with her hand.

"What? I didn't say anything to him."

"He didn't," Davis agreed. "Charlie told me what she found about buried gold. I think she wanted you to find some as much as you did."

They all laughed.

"And hey," Davis said as he grabbed his champagne glass once more. "You may not have found gold, but you found each other, which is even better. Cheers to the happy couple!"

They all clinked glasses or hot chocolate mugs in Sadie's case.

"Cheers!"

Charlie was right. It was Sadie's wedding celebration. Well, a double one, really. She and JoJo decided on a double ceremony earlier in the month, just them at the church with only family. Charlie was Sadie's matron of honor, and Mark was James' best man. Maddie was there, of course, but they all wanted something intimate, something quiet. Charlie was the one who insisted on throwing a big party to celebrate, and now Sadie could see why. This was her family, this community. She and JoJo had been loved and supported for longer than they realized.

She'd moved in with him and Maddie right after the wedding. Gary had moved in with JoJo as planned. After they got engaged, James said he wanted to help her pay the difference in rent at the store. It wasn't easy at first for Sadie to receive that, but JoJo reminded her they both needed to work on receiving as much as giving. And James had said if he couldn't spend what he'd made in the NFL on his gorgeous wife, what was it good for? How could Sadie refuse that?

James looked her way and smiled.

They were a team now. A family. And Sadie couldn't think of a better Christmas present than that.

The End

ACKNOWLEDGMENTS

So much goes on behind the scenes to create a book. Yes, the writing is key, but there is so much more beyond that. People who work hard, encourage, and make the journey possible from idea to actual book form.

Thank you, Crystal Posey, for being my literal right hand. For gorgeous book covers, formatting, marketing, and basically keeping me on track, sane, and making it fun to get up each day and do this writing gig. Your constant encouragement means the world to me. You are truly the best.

Thank you, Laura Shin. Editing is my least favorite part of this process and you honestly make it fun for me (which is saying a lot). I greatly appreciate your flexibility with my schedule and how you make the process seamless and enjoyable.

The ECC Quilting group. Thank you for welcoming me into the fold when I came to you with a simple desire to learn how to quilt yet had never sewn before in my life and didn't own a sewing machine. Your kindness, your laughter, your friendship has become a most cherished community to me, and I adore you all.

My family. Thank you for listening as I verbally processed characters and story. Thank you for making research fun. Thank you for your patience with me during the writing process when I hole up for hours in my office and for all the years you have been my biggest cheerleaders. I love you bunches.

ABOUT THE AUTHOR

 Writing stories since she was a young girl, Lara's dream of being a novelist became a reality with her Men of Honor series. An avid reader, she worked as a book reviewer for 18 years with various organizations. She has a BA in Journalism and a Masters of Divinity in Chaplaincy. Lara loves tea, baseball and living in Idaho with her husband and Great Dane. You can find Lara online at www.laramvanhulzen.com

ALSO BY LARA

The Endicotts of Silver Bay Series
Love at Meg's Diner, Book One
Christmas Cakes and Kisses, Book Two
Until I Met You, Book Three
An Angel for Christmas, Book Four

The Silver Bay Series
Return to Silver Bay, Book One
Loving Kate, Book Two
Saving Drew, Book Three
Hannah's Hope, A Novella

The Marietta St. Claire Series
A Recipe for Romance, Book One
Winning His Heart, Book Two
His Christmas Bride, Book Three
Finding Her Montana Cowboy, Book Four

The Men of Honor Series
Remember Me, Book One
Get to Me, Book Two
Rescue Me, Book Three

Single Titles
I Grew Up Dancing: Celebrating the Joy of Knowing Jesus
(daily devotional)
Guarding Paragon (young adult fiction)

Made in United States
Troutdale, OR
10/22/2024

24044761R00152